MW00874363

A GLASS
HALF
EMPTY

NATHAN BAINE

ARCHWAY
PUBLISHING

Copyright © 2020 Nathan Baine.

All rights reserved. No part of this book may be used or reproduced by any means, graphic, electronic, or mechanical, including photocopying, recording, taping or by any information storage retrieval system without the written permission of the author except in the case of brief quotations embodied in critical articles and reviews.

This is a work of fiction. All of the characters, names, incidents, organizations, and dialogue in this novel are either the products of the author's imagination or are used fictitiously.

Archway Publishing books may be ordered through booksellers or by contacting:

Archway Publishing
1663 Liberty Drive
Bloomington, IN 47403
www.archwaypublishing.com
844-669-3957

Because of the dynamic nature of the Internet, any web addresses or links contained in this book may have changed since publication and may no longer be valid. The views expressed in this work are solely those of the author and do not necessarily reflect the views of the publisher, and the publisher hereby disclaims any responsibility for them.

Any people depicted in stock imagery provided by Getty Images are models, and such images are being used for illustrative purposes only. Certain stock imagery © Getty Images.

ISBN: 978-1-4808-9893-6 (sc)
ISBN: 978-1-4808-9909-4 (e)

Library of Congress Control Number: 2020921626

Print information available on the last page.

Archway Publishing rev. date: 11/02/2020

For Molly

The cat walks across my belly. It's 11:00 a.m. and time to wake up, I guess. I swipe my arm, gently, at the black cat, signaling him to leap from my stomach. I'm too hungover to have a ten-pound creature resting upon my navel this morning. He looks up at me, pissed, from the side of the bed. Not as pissed as I was yesterday. Though I admire his glare—for someone who can't speak, his eyes tell a story. And that story today is "fuck you, asshole." I understand. I'll accept his affection later. But for now, I need isolation. Physical and mental. At least until noon. That's when the bar reopens.

Another long night, another day. My head throbs, and there's an uneasy feeling in my gut. Nauseous but not quite queasy enough to vomit, I roll off my back and sit on the edge of the bed. I run my hands over my face and hair, attempting to recall what happened after I left the bar last night—or early this morning, to be technical. I try not to be technical, living this lifestyle. Technicalities only muddy the waters of the conscience and leave one questioning. I don't ask questions I don't want the answers to. Pass.

Barrrragh! I burp loudly. That felt good.

I'm surprised I didn't puke. It's difficult to gauge belches at this time of morning. It's even more of a struggle to trust belches later in the night. A belly full of drink can cause a man to expel a gastro-nomical movement followed by chunky stomach acid or, even worse, the remnants of the evening's alcohol intake. Waste of money, if you ask me. I even regard urinating in a watering hole as a literal pissing away of money—which is why I rarely visit a public restroom. *Fuck 'em,* I think. If I'm paying premium prices for drinks, I'm going to soak up the lot. Not a drop wasted. Every penny earned.

I rise up onto my feet, standing slowly so as not to allow the blood to rush to my head. I used to arise too quickly, until the time I found myself in the emergency room with six stitches after I passed out upright and smacked my head on the bathroom door while relieving myself in the toilet. Puddles of blood everywhere. Believe me, sitting in a hospital waiting room covered in type O and urine is no way to go through a Thursday. Though there are worse fates. I could work in sanitation on my day-to-day.

Walking to the bathroom of this one-bedroom apartment, I realize how cozy my nest has become, with the exception of a collec-tion of *Rolling Stone* magazines nestled in the corner of my bedroom, which I amassed, beginning in my youth, from 1999 to the present. The rest of the apartment is filled with essentials—groceries, beer, whiskey, records, television, couch.

I'm appreciating my place more now, considering I haven't worked in a couple months and have been blowing through my savings to remain afloat. *This could all be gone tomorrow,* I think. And then what? I could move back in with my parents, but at my age—thirty—that would mean resigning myself to the fact that I might not get laid again until I earned enough cash for a security de-posit and first month's rent on a new place—most likely in an awful neighborhood. Something I have grown out of, despite only working minimum-wage, manual-labor jobs for the last eight or so years. Fuck it, I'll figure it out another day. For now, I just need to piss.

I reach the toilet and sit down. I always sit when I pee in the mornings. Two reasons—I am ill-equipped to stand at this juncture, and the piss boner I'm nursing will spray in only one direction (the one I'm not aiming). I listen to the liquid stream from my urethra into the bowl. Sweet relief.

I notice my lower abdomen, around the location of my bladder, decrease in size and the swelling from the urine draining out of my system. Down, down, down, until the surface under my naval is left visibly flatter.

I flush the toilet and pull my boxers up around my waist. Noticing dribbles of urine on the seat, I wipe the penile leakage from the surface with toilet paper and toss it in the trash bin. On the bathroom counter sit two framed photos. The first photograph is of my sisters and me when all seven of us were in our early to late twenties. It's a reference to a past that featured joyous, confident faces looking toward a promising future that never was. The second photograph shows a group of my childhood friends, dating back to our high school years. Not all the souls in these photographs are still among the living. As I look into the eyes of the now deceased, I am reminded that, one day, all of us will be nothing more than faces in a photograph. Entombed on paper behind glass as nothing more than a memory of past generations.

I quickly glance in the mirror and, in an attempt to be presentable, comb back my brownish auburn hair. I consider shaving, but the thought leaves as fast as it came. Normally, I'm self-conscious about my beard growing out and exposing my ginger facial hair, but there's only a little stubble this morning. It will be fine for now.

I exit the lavatory and make my way into the kitchen, where I pour a tall glass of water, followed by a rapid chugging. Hydration for the day. Breathing heavily, I pour another glass of water and begin to sip it reluctantly. Nothing tastes good to me in the morning except for water. There are only two remedies for this ailment—the aforementioned numerous glasses of water and the first alcoholic drink of the day. I hope to have the latter very soon.

My nose feels stuffed up, and I snort the snot back up and down into my throat, hocking up the loogie into my mouth. I hold the wad of mucus in my mouth and return to the bathroom to spit into the sink. I wash away the loogie, watching it swirl down the drain. I glance at the photographs on the countertop again and reflect on my friendships. I have a few left. And the ones I do are always waiting for me between noon and 2:00 a.m. I'll see them there.

Finally I'm dressed and ready to walk out the door in my usual costume—tight blue jeans and an Arcade Fire t-shirt. Hand-me-downs from high school. I handed them down to my adult self. Not much has changed in size, so good enough for me. Perhaps it's an attempt to capture past youth, but aren't we all? No beer has ever tasted as good as the first, no fuck has felt as good as the first, no album has ever sounded as good as the first, and no meal has tasted as good as the first time sipping milk from your mother's teat. It's all about nourishment. That's what connects Americans to inhabitants of third world countries. We all need nourishment. And those types are the most memorable.

I grab my keys and walk out the door, nudging my cat away with my foot so as not to let him escape. I shut and lock the door and turn the handle to make sure the deadbolt is secure. Clipping the carabiner on my key chain to my belt loop, I stroll down the hallway toward the elevator.

2

Riding the elevator down to the lobby, I'm accompanied by an older woman with two Pomeranians on leashes. They stare at me and bark.

"I'm sorry. They're a bit wound up today."

"It's fine."

The dogs walk up to my shoes and sniff. They're quiet for a moment and bark again as the doors open to the lobby floor.

"Sorry again."

"No worries. I'm sure they smell my pussy."

The old woman glares at me disapprovingly and ushers her bitches off the elevator. I can't blame her. Cats aren't for everyone.

I exit the lobby doors of the apartment complex and pace south toward the bar. I've always loved walks. They give me time to think and meditate before beginning each day. Solace from all the entrapments of life, love, relationships, employment, and so on. The only responsibilities are that of the road. I wait for the crosswalk signs to signal me forward. I stroll into the street, feeling each step hit the pavement beneath me in pedestrian unison. Rhythmically, I stride across to the opposing sidewalk like a man on a mission. My task? Make this day more memorable than the last. Not an easy challenge, considering I can't recall much of the previous evening. Therefore, it must've been more noteworthy than I can rightly give it credit for.

I stare disdainfully at my surroundings. The yuppies, the house-wives, the SUVs, the minivans, the chain restaurants, the malls—my whole neighborhood looks like a suburban outlet with a barely beating pulse. The only hope is a MARTA train station that can have you within Atlanta city limits in a matter of minutes. I like knowing there's an escape route if necessary. But lately I haven't needed one. I've found my place within a neighborhood pub located in a strip mall, next to a movie theater and a Home Goods. It's suited me well for now.

I approach the bar. I can see the sign in front. It reads "Royal Tree" but it might as well say "Home." I reach the entrance only to be deflected by a nonilluminated closed sign. I check my watch—11:55 a.m. Five more minutes. I'll wait outside.

I light a cigarette from a pack I picked up the night before. It's an American Spirit, my least favorite brand. It's not personal or meant to be unpatriotic on my part. They just smoke too slowly for my taste. The burn is unhurried and fades, like an artist who continues output past his or her prime. *It's better to burn out than fade away.* I read that in a suicide note once.

Five minutes later, I see Tyler, the afternoon bartender, turn on the sign and open the door. She's an attractive girl—pretty faced, busty, early thirties. She's been a Royal Tree staple for some years. Hard to say for sure. I know she was once a regular before joining the staff as the afternoon bar tender roughly four years ago. Her first day tending bar closely coincided with my first day on the other side of the bar. Rumor has it, she's leaving in the coming weeks to take a position as manager of a sister bar across town. Need to enjoy our time while it lasts. She greets me.

"Hello, Matt!"

"Hello, Tyler."

"How's it going?"

"Spectacular. You?"

"Just another day in paradise."

I love a bartender's sarcasm. They see people as they truly are and make the best of the ugliness. Such an optimistic way to go through life. I wish I could see the world through those lenses. Though it would take a monumental injection of promising hope to correct my optics on life at this point.

I flick the remainder of my cigarette onto the street behind me, watching it twist and turn gracefully midair. I think of Tony Hawk landing the 900. Impressive. Moments in time. I may never dispose of anything in quite a fashion again. Too bad there isn't an audience. If there were, I'm sure a bystander would pass me another cigarette to watch me smoke it and discard of the butt in a similar way. Best case scenario. I don't count on it. The greatest art usually goes unnoticed anyways.

I walk across the threshold and officially enter the pub. I'm the first one here. An endless option of seats for the day. I choose a stool at the bar in front of the TV. Victory.

The pub is dimly lit. Most of the light comes from rays of sun peaking in from the windows and glass front door. There's not much to the place. Nothing particularly special or unordinary. Dark wood stained booths, tables, and bar top make up most of the room. A couple of TVs are mounted on the walls—one behind the bar and another hanging in the dining area. The revolving channels consist of ESPN, Fox Sports, Fox News, CNN, or whatever Atlanta-based sporting event is happening at the moment. Sports is always a reliable source of entertainment at a bar. But when it comes to the news, I can't help but think of the old adage, "Best not to discuss politics when people have been drinking." I find that to be the best time to discuss politics. That's when folks are loose and let their opinions fly. It's nice to see others get riled up. Which is why, late at night after the games have ended, I occasionally suggest tuning one TV to Fox News and the other to CNN. Really gets the blood boiling.

There's a Golden Tee arcade game in the corner. Across from the arcade game is a dart board with a scoring chart. The ceiling is also a black chalkboard base where past visitors and regulars sign with various colors of chalk, signifying their existence at one point or another. A friend of mine, Raj, once proposed to his girlfriend here with a written "Marry Me?" chalk inscription on the ceiling. It took some effort to get his future wife to stare up at the heavens in order to see his proposal. That was a great night. Free drinks for the regulars and an impromptu party ensued. Good times.

My favorite attribute of the pub, however, is the jukebox. Nested nicely in the back of the pub, near the bathroom, it provides the majority of the late-night entertainment. Once there was a cigarette machine in its place, which was pleasurable. Then that was removed and replaced with an old-timey jukebox, *Happy Days* style. Every time a dollar was inserted into it, I could almost feel my inner Fonzie take over. It was loaded with CDs from artists of the '80s and '90s and modern country *sangers*. After the locals had their way with the machine, it was decided in the bar's best interest by management to upgrade to a digital jukebox, offering any number of songs at the user's fingertips at any moment, and I've been known to insert a few dollars in now and then, despite my resentment for the futuristic addition to the pub. It's not that it wasn't convenient. The digital jukebox just took away from the pub's charm. The joint was essentially a dive located in a suburban dystopia, signifying a bygone era where drinks were cheap, mouths were foul, and the sounds remained the same.

An old-style jukebox provided the soundtrack of life for the locals. Changing out the soundtrack for a wide array of music is like if *Pulp Fiction* was reedited to not include the "Misirlou" by Dick Dale & His Del-Tones or any Scorsese movie went without a Rolling Stones track. It just wouldn't be the same. Instead, now, the digital jukebox provided entertainment for anyone who visited the bar. Anyone could have a good time. And as accessible as this may be for

John Q. Public and as profitable as it may be for the owners, it was equally as upsetting to the regulars. This place wasn't for the public. It was for us—the barflies glued to the walls, unable to let go from their grip. And now, we were left to endure a song that wasn't written for us. Our outsourcing in favor of a nihilistic clientele had begun. Character was fleeting. But thank God some of us remembered the old tunes. And when it was our turn, we played them long enough to drive away the riffraff.

I stand up from my seat before Tyler can reach me to take my order and introduce myself to the digital jukebox for the day, putting in a dollar for two songs. I search the online database for my choices and come up with a couple of solid opening numbers. "Dry the Rain" by the Beta Band and "For What It's Worth" by Buffalo Springfield. Let's set the tone for the day.

Tyler is behind the bar, still prepping for her afternoon shift. She empties the dishwasher from the previous night and stacks the pint glasses along the wall near the beer taps and liquor display. I wonder how many of those glasses had been drunk by me at some point the night prior? In an effort to remain in a state of denial, I throw the thought away.

I ask Tyler for my opening beverage. A pint of Guinness. Something tells me a long night is ahead. Best to start slow.

It's 12:30 p.m. I finish my first pint of Guinness. Might as well have another.

"Tyler, could I have another?"

"Sure."

Tyler struts to the draft display and pours the pint. Properly. There's an art to pouring a pint of Guinness. Straight down. Slowly. And leaving just enough head to level off the glass top. Tyler successfully completes this task. A pro. A veteran. Seasoned, she is. She delivers the glass of beer to me. I wait for the yeast to settle, turning the liquid a stark black color before taking the initial sip. How joyous that initial sip if beer is. After the initial gulp, all problems seem to fade like a disposable acquaintance. And among barfly culture, they are plentiful.

I take a second sip from the pint glass. This time, it's more of a gulp than a sip. The more I taste, the more I desire another. I believe junkies refer to this as "chasing the dragon." Poor bastards. I feel for them. Though, after I switch gears later to whiskey, I've been known to breathe fire on occasion. Fuck chasing the dragon. I'll become the dragon instead. At that point, I'll no longer be a slave to the drug. I'll be the master. Then no one can fuck with me. Not that I'll be looking for trouble. Drink rarely makes me an angry bastard. A tad mouthy, but that's just the courage seeping out. It's the "liquid courage" an amateur drinker may reference. A professional drinker would never use this phrase, for he or she is aware of its falsehood. Seasoned drinkers don't indulge to gain courage. They drink to hide out of fear. Fear of the truth. Fear of the world. Fear of their reality. To do this takes courage. The willingness to face oneself head-on every day takes balls. And it's that fortitude that allows one to drink. To escape. To rewrite the script. Not forever but for a moment. Courage comes before the first order.

I continue to sip at the Guinness, occasionally gazing peripherally to see what Tyler is up to. I'm curious when I'm lonely. I'm sure that's what has led me to venturing to bars on solo missions these past years. I've yet to hold a steady relationship of late to keep me company at night. They come and go and always leave me wishing they'd have ended sooner than they lasted. It's not that there is a lack of effort on my part. Just haven't found the right fit. It's like trying on numerous pairs of jeans, searching for the right size and cut to fit.

Some may say I'm particular, but it's the details that interest me. What are we without details and multitudes? Just another face in a crowd? Another wave in a sea of forgettable tides? In my case, more often than not, it's the woman who terminates the engagement. Various reasons have been explained to me, but I always suspect another suitor has entered the picture, leaving me the odd one out. I most recently was left by a woman for a Mexican man named Antonio Banderas. Like the actor. Not saying I'm bitter, but I haven't watched another one of the actor's films since. Fuck Zorro.

In addition to being left for other men, I also have found myself dumped on holidays as well. Valentine's Day, Christmas, New Year's Eve. At this rate, I may have better luck meeting someone on Tax Day.

Now I'm feeling hunger pains. I haven't eaten since 6:00 p.m. yesterday, and all I have left in my belly are mozzarella sticks that

I've most assuredly digested by now. I check my watch—12:51 p.m. Time for lunch.

"Tyler, can I get a menu?"

Tyler halts stacking glasses and approaches me, holding a menu that is printed to resemble a newspaper. A nice touch. Though considering the addition of the digital jukebox, I wouldn't be surprised if iPads were distributed to customers as a substitute for traditional menus. When that day comes, I'll probably find myself drinking sake and Sapporo at a sushi bar instead. At least they have the audacity to stick to a paper menu.

"Here ya go."

"Thanks."

I peruse the menu—flipping the pages back and forth like my grandfather used to in search of the sports section or the funnies. A sandwich. That will do for now.

"Tyler, I'm ready to order."

"What'll you have?"

"I'm gonna go with the chicken Tuscan sandwich. No mayo."

"Side?"

"Veggies."

"Going with the healthy option today, I see."

"Always. It takes discipline to keep this ass in business."

"I didn't know you were for sale."

"We're all for sale, Tyler. It just depends on the price."

"And your price being?"

"All depends on the market."

"Well, hopefully we have some customers today besides you. There's a Braves game on later, so that might attract some business."

"Let us hope. I'd hate to be here all day with just the two of us."

"Gee, thanks, Matt."

"Don't take it personal, Tyler. You know you're my favorite person here right now."

"Funny."

Tyler takes the menu from me and walks to the register to input my lunch order into the pub's computer system.

"Oh, Tyler!"

"Yup?"

"Another Guinness while you're over there."

"Sure thing."

"Appreciate it. Also, can you turn on ESPN when you get the chance?"

"I gotcha."

Tyler pours my third pint and tunes the flat screen to ESPN. *SportsCenter* is on. That'll keep me preoccupied until my friends arrive.

I finish my third Guinness as Tyler delivers my Tuscan sandwich.
"Tuscan sandwich with steamed veggies. Anything else?"

"No. That'll be all for now. Thanks."

"No problem."

Once Tyler walks away, I proceed to devour my meal while no
one is in eyeshot. Before the food is done steaming, I've already en-
gulfed it and am in the process of digestion. My tongue burns and
blisters from the heat of the chicken and pesto sauce. I'm regretting
having finished my beer in this moment, for a swig would do me
good at this juncture. Why the fuck did I not let my food cool down?

I know why. Fear of Tyler or an incoming patron catching me
enjoying the plate.

I'm not a fan of people watching me eat. I find eating a very
personal thing—on par with shitting and masturbating and sex.
You learn a lot about people when observing how they defecate or
feast or fuck. Vulnerability shines through during these activities.
I don't find weakness in vulnerability. Quite the contrary. It takes
a certain level of strength to allow others to watch you consume. I
just personally haven't developed a level of self-confidence to open
myself up in this way. Which would explain my fascination with

watching the Nathan's Hot Dog Eating Contest or listening to Louis C. K. discuss jerking off in front of women for pleasure. I realize the strength it requires to expose oneself. Fascinating. Someday I only hope to have the ability to muster the vigor of a Joey Chestnut. For now, I'll have a cigarette and order another drink.

I push my empty plate away. I'm slightly disgusted by how quickly I finished. It's similar to the feeling of bedding a woman only to come too soon. Ashamed. I need to forget. I stand up from the barstool and signal to garner Tyler's attention. She notices me, and her eyebrows raise in acknowledgment.

"Tyler, I'm gonna step outside for a sec."

"Okay. No problem."

"Could I also get another Guinness?"

"Yeah, I'll have that waiting for you when you come back in."

"Awesome. Thanks, Tyler."

I turn away and walk out the front door for the open-air patio. The sun is shining and a cool, gentle summer breeze is blowing. I pull an American Spirit from the pack holstered in my back pocket. Three more remain. I put the cigarette between my lips and pull the lighter from my front pocket, lighting the tip while cupping my hands in front of my face, preventing the wind from blowing out the blue ignited flame. It's lit. I take a long inhale from the hot stick and exhale the smoke from my lungs. A smoke after a meal. As classic as Coca-Cola on the Fourth of July.

I continue smoking my American Spirit, all the while ruminating on my disdain for the brand. Natural tobacco never burns quite like the chemical-infused mainstream cigarettes. On the plus side, if a tumor metastasizes in my lungs or throat it will be non-GMO and organic. I'm sure a crunchy, granola medicine man will one day tell me the cure for the disease consists of elderberry syrup and an Eckhart Tolle reading.

As I exhale another cloud of carcinogens from my lungs, I see Dane approaching from the parking lot. I knew he'd be here. He looks the same as he always does—short, heavyset, middle-aged (roughly fifteen years older than me), Washington Nationals ball cap, fleece, and baggy blue jeans. He reaches the patio of the Royal Tree.

"Hey, Matt!"

"Afternoon, Dane."

"How's it going?"

"Same as yesterday."

"Ha! Well given how last night went, I'm surprised to see you here."

"I'm like herpes, Dane. I'm always here."

"Well, nice to see you flare up, I guess."

I laugh at the retort.

"Let me grab a drink, and I'll come out and join you."

"Sounds good."

Dane walks inside and leaves me outside to smoke alone, momentarily. No worries. Dane smokes Camel Crush, which, when it comes to longevity, is no match for the American Spirits I'm holding. He'll catch up in no time.

Dane emerges from the pub with a Bloody Mary. He sits his Bloody Mary on a high-top table on the patio and removes his pack of Camel Crush from his fleece pocket. He lights up. Dane exhales and takes a drink of the red vegetable-based liquid.

"So, Matt, how are you feeling today?"

"Not bad. Better than I did a couple of hours ago. You?"

"Ah, I'm fine now. I made breakfast this morning around 6:00 a.m. and felt a hundred times better after that."

"At 6:00 a.m.? Why the hell did you get up that early?"

"Ha. I always do. I can't help it. I just rise early."

"What time did you leave last night?"

"Same time as you. I drove you home."

"You did?"

"You don't remember that?"

"Dane, I don't remember shit past midnight."

"Ha ha. Wow, okay. Do you remember getting that girl's number?"

"What girl?"

"Jesus, how fucked up were you? Ha ha."

"It's hard to judge these things, Dane."

"Well, before we left, you were talking to this real cute girl at the bar. She was hanging out with friends of hers, and y'all started talking about a book you were reading last night."

"Oh, *High Fidelity*?"

"Fuck if I know what book it was. If that's what you're reading, then I assume that's the one."

"Oh shit! Yeah, that's right. I remember now. Real cute? Blonde, curly hair?"

"Yup! That's the one. Probably twenty-five or so."

"Yeah, sorry. I just needed to jar my brain. My memory has turned to shit. Hmm. I'll have to check my phone and see if I took the number."

I check my phone and look through my recent calls from the night before, checking to make sure I didn't ring the lady. There it is. It's the third number in my recent calls list, just behind Bob and Ernie. I'm guessing I called her and immediately hung up so I'd have her number saved in my phone. It's followed by later-night calls to Bob and Ernie after I got home. Probably to discuss a recent film I saw or rave about the complexities of a new album we'd been all been listening to. Common talking points with them as of late.

I see her number saved in my phone as "Holly Royal Tree." I have to save people's numbers in my phone based on their first name with the last name being the place I met them. Nervously, I check to make sure I didn't drunkenly text her last night. Nothing. I'm in the clear. Thank Christ. Don't want to scare this one away too early. Now that my memory is coming back to me, I recall our encounter and remember she was quite interesting and beautiful. Maybe I'll text her later today. Worth a shot. Could lead to something. Or nothing. Either way, I'll be here.

I remember Dane is still standing next to me as I examine my phone. "Sorry. Just wanted to make sure I didn't drunk dial anyone last night."

"Hey, no worries."

"You gonna watch the Braves game later?"

"Yeah, they're playing the Mets, right?"

"I think so."

"That should be a good rivalry game."

"Yeah, hopefully. I wouldn't mind seeing the Bravos smoke their asses."

"Yeah, we'll see."

Dane and I both finish our cigarettes around the same time. Dane puts his out in an ashtray on the high-top housing his Bloody Mary. I flick mine onto the street. We walk back into the Royal Tree. I'm glad he made it out this early. No one likes to drink and smoke alone. Even though I don't mind it. But it's the weekend, and this is a time for celebrating.

The afternoon sunshine peaks through into the pub, brightening the room up even more so than it had an hour ago. A beam of light shines through the door, illuminating the pint of beer waiting for me at the bar. Must be a sign.

I'm sitting at the bar atop my previous stool. My throne for a day. Seems fitting. I've learned of kings with less esteem than me.

Now onto my fourth pint of Guinness. I slowly sip the beer, savoring the flavor now. I notice a slight buzz running through my body from the beer, punctuated by the previous cigarette. As the alcohol courses through my system, I can't help but notice an intense itching along my lower legs. I lift my pant leg up to check what's the matter. Goddamn eczema is flaring up again.

"Fuck me," I mutter to myself.

I scratch. Furiously. However, this doesn't do much by way of curing the problem. If anything, a good grazing of the fingernails over the rash only temporarily alleviates the itch. A Band-Aid for an open wound. It'll have to do for now. Best to continue drinking and hope to numb the irritation until I can return home and apply dabs of the Gold Bond ointment I keep under the sink, right next to the first aid kit and plunger.

I hate when this epidermal affliction takes shape—often during times of stress. Though I can't seem to understand what would bring the stress on. It's definitely not work-related. I haven't had a steady job in months. This isn't due to job performance, so much as a communication breakdown or unwillingness to conform to the time structures dictated by management. I've had a history of employment terminations the last couple of years.

First, I was let go from a landscaping job for "falsifying my time cards" according to payroll. Apparently, it's not considered labor hours during the commute to and from work. As far as I am concerned, though, the work day begins when I get in my car to drive to the job site that morning, and it extends through the commute home from said job site. If I am devoting my time in any way to an employer, I expect to see the dividends.

The next was a construction job performing demolition work in an old produce storage facility. It was more of a deconstruction job, in my opinion. I like the sound of that better. I'd found it more enjoyable to destroy than create, ever since I learned I lacked a certain artistic touch. Found that out the hard way after a number of screenplays I had written in college were turned down by agents and studios alike. Nothing like shattered dreams to alter one's perspective on the world.

The demolition work was fine though. I quite enjoyed swinging a sledgehammer and transporting rubble to large dumpsters via a forklift. The boss on this particular job site, Mitch, was a fairly cool guy and didn't seem to mind me playing music in the warehouse on my portable stereo or even having a beer at lunch. He tended to look the other way, so as long as the crew I worked with gutted the building in a timely fashion and saved the loose copper pipes and wiring for him to sell at a premium to scrap yards. Only thing that was not tolerated was tardiness or not showing up at all. Which I learned the hard way earlier this summer.

One Thursday night in mid-June after work, I found myself at an old pub called The Colony in midtown with my cousin, Bo. It was just two miles away from my apartment, at the time, and around midnight we decided to head home to have some post-bar night drinks at my place. We had a good old-fashioned drunk, listened to records, and rehashed past stories from our youth. Eventually we passed out in the living room. Empty beer cans surrounded our bodies, overhead lights were fully illuminated, and scraps of dried-up Rotel cheese dip were left out on the kitchen counter from a well-past-midnight snacking. I awakened to high noon sunlight beaming in from the window, offensively hitting me in the face with the force of a boot to the head. I checked my watch and observed it was well past 2:00 pm, making me roughly six hours late to work. I got off the couch, still wearing a short-sleeve Hawaiian button-up shirt and jeans from the night before, and hauled ass in my '94 Yukon to the produce facility, where I was greeted by Mitch and his merry band of day laborers I had been working alongside.

"Hey, Mitch. Sorry I'm late."

"Do you realize what fucking time it is, Matt?"

I checked the time. Head throbbing from a hangover, it was difficult to read the hands of my watch. "Looks like it's about 2:30 p.m."

"Yeah, no shit! You were supposed to be here at 8:00 a.m.!"

"Yeah sorry about that. I lost track of time."

"Lost track of time for over six hours? How the fuck does that happen?"

I searched for a reasonable excuse. "I was at the Juneteenth parade."

I could tell by the look in his eyes that this fable infuriated Mitch beyond comprehension. I guess he wasn't as big a fan of African American independence celebrations and jazz as I was.

"You know what? We don't need you today. Or any day from here on. You're fired! So, take your ass on home or back to the parade. I don't give a shit what you do!"

Mitch walked away, and I had to ask. "Can I get my check for this week before I go?"

Mitch turned around, fuming with annoyance, and stared at me long and hard. And then he took out his checkbook and wrote me what I was due for the previous hours of work that week. I read the check—amount, "$256.00"; subject line, "for work not completed." I still thought I should've been paid for the drive time there that day. But I guessed I'd take it, I figured.

I continue to sit at the bar in Royal Tree, periodically scratching the eczema breakout on my right leg with my left foot. "Goddamn it, I'm tired of this shit," I say. I take longer pulls from the pint glass and quickly finish my beer in just two more gulps. The booze masks some of the itching, but I know it will return. Afflictions always come back. I'll have to slow this breakout somehow. Better have a shot of Jameson to get the creative juices flowing. But given my lack thereof, I may just have to obliterate the sore instead.

I signal to Tyler to order a shooter.

"What's up?"

"Can I get a shot of Jameson with a Coke back?"

"Yes, ma'am."

Funny. I don't mind the slight. The irritation on my leg is so severe, I don't care about anything except for having the shot of Irish whiskey and soda delivered as soon as possible. Tyler returns in less than a minute with a glass of Coca-Cola and a single shot of Jameson. I'd have preferred a double, but I'll let it slide.

"Here ya go."

"Thanks, Tyler. I appreciate it."

Tyler walks away, and I shoot the whiskey down my gullet, feeling the burning sensation tickle my throat on the way south into my stomach lining. I sit the shot glass down on the bar top and lift the glass of Coke up to my lips and take a large gulp. The sugary corn syrup coats my throat and is soothing. My leg still itches. Hopefully a few more drinks will scratch it from the inside.

6

Dane and I sit next to each other at the bar. Dane enjoying large samples from his scotch and water. Me, onto my fifth Guinness. A strong feeling of elation washing over me, warming my body even more than the toasty summer air.

Dane looks up from his drink to find Tyler with his eyes. "Tyler? Could I order some food please?"

"Sure thing. What would you like?"

"I'll have the double burger with a side of fries."

"Simple enough. I'll have that right out."

Tyler walks away to the kitchen, announcing Dane's order to the cooks. No need to type it into the system. No other customers are in the pub now, except for Dane and me.

Roughly ten minutes later, Dane's burger and fries arrive in front of him.

"Thanks Tyler!"

"No problem. Ketchup? Mustard?"

"Ketchup, please."

Tyler hands Dane a bottle of Ketchup. He squeezes the condiment all over his fries and the inside of his burger bun. Dane enjoys his burger at a vastly slower rate than I handled the Tuscan sandwich. He holds off on the fries as well—letting those cool down before partaking. He's in no hurry. His breakfast earlier is tiding him over quite well.

I am glad Dane is here. His presence is familiar, as he's been a known figure of the Royal Tree since long before I showed up on the scene. He's a veteran drinker and one of the first patrons to take me under his wing when I began frequenting the pub. Back then, I considered myself a pro. But after meeting Dane. I soon learned I was only minor league—not quite a rookie but definitely not ready to play with the big boys. Given his tutelage and my willingness to match him drink for drink, I earned my stripes. A few months later, I was in the show.

I consider Dane a friend—and I haven't many—one worth keeping in touch with. Even should a dismal event happen, forcing the Royal Tree to close its doors for good, I would still want to keep him as a drinking buddy. The man can lead a good conversation and is always game to stay well past when we should be leaving. He's a trooper. I'm happy to share a foxhole with him. Not that we're engaging in combat or a physical war. But we're definitely fighting an existential battle. Every day, we're awarded our own purple hearts for emotional or psychological injuries.

Dane's story was one consisting of multiple monumental heartbreaks. Two marriages under his belt and still hung up on his most recent ex-wife, Matilda. She left him last year for reasons that remain a mystery to me to this day. Dane rarely speaks of the divorce and chooses to only discuss the potential for them to rekindle their relationship at a later date. *Good luck*, I think. But I won't hold my breath. Anyway, his first marriage was an even more disturbing situation than I could imagine and overshadowed his second marriage like an eclipse.

His first marriage ended when his wife passed away in a tragic drowning accident. From what I recall, though my memory is fuzzier than channel 99 on an old tube TV, she fell into a churning river and was carried downstream out of sight and far from shore. Dane saw it all. The current was too strong to retrieve her, and within seconds, she was out of sight. Forever.

Dane could barely keep his composure when he first told me the story. Poor guy. I felt awful for him and bought him enough shots that evening to forget, if only for a couple of hours. After, I picked up his tab. Sometimes a small gesture can go a long way for someone in distress. Dane seemed eternally thankful to me for picking up his tab and decided to pay me back over the years by supplying me with an endless number of free cigarettes whenever I was running low.

Dane finishes his burger and fries and wipes the grease from the corners of his mouth. I continue on with my beer. Dane orders another scotch and water. Tyler, standing behind the bar, makes the cocktail. She gives Dane a heavy pour of Johnnie Walker Red at no extra charge. A perk of being a long-standing patron of the Royal Tree. He's earned it. Tyler sprays a couple of splashes of water into the glass before dropping in a plastic straw and delivering Dane his drink.

Royal Tree is one of the few bars remaining that still carries plastic straws and not the new paper-based alternative—something I can tell the regulars appreciate. Paper straws are used with good intentions. Save the environment, save the turtles, all that shit. But they're a vastly inferior form of liquid delivery system. Sure, you can slam your drink down and have little to worry about. But if you choose to drink at a normal pace, you'll eventually be left with essentially a disintegrated floating napkin that once resembled a straw in your glass. Fuck off. No one wants that in his or her life. Fuck the environment. Fuck the turtles. Give me a plastic straw and find another eco-friendly solution for the earth that doesn't interrupt my vice of choice.

Dane drinks his cocktails in an interesting way. He likes to have a plastic straw in his drink, though he chooses not to use it as intended. Instead he bends the straw back over the back of the glass, takes a swig, and uses the deformed plastic to mix the ice throughout the cocktail. Peculiar.

"Dane, what time is the game on today?"

"Let me check."

Dane takes out his iPhone and opens the ESPN app to find the schedule. "Looks like it's starting at 3:30 p.m. today."

"Huh, that's unusual. They usually throw the first pitch out around 1:00 p.m. or 7:00 p.m."

"Yeah, but the game is being played in New York, so I think it's to line up with the TV airing."

"Well, looks like we got some time before the game starts. Wanna step outside for a smoke?"

"Sure, I'll go out there with ya."

"Let's do it to it, Lars."

Dane and I step away from the bar, drinks in hand, and walk outside to the pub patio and light up. I can tell Dane appreciates a cigarette after a meal as much I do. He slowly exhales the smoke from his mouth and sighs deeply in enjoyment. It's nice to see him take pleasure in little things after all he's been through.

I take a look around outside at the parking lot, now filling with cars and shoppers and matinee moviegoers alike. The sun beams down upon us, and it feels rejuvenating. Like a shot of vitamins in the buttocks.

It's such a fine day. We can't waste it inside completely. Thank God for smoke breaks. They really let people get some fresh air.

7

Outside the Royal Tree, on the patio, Dane has ashed out his Camel Crush and retreated back to his domicile for the day. I continue to take drags off an American Spirit, desperate to reach the filter. American Spirits feel like an anxiety test for me while smoking them. These damn things should come with a Prozac prescription, I think. All I want is to finish one and feel satisfied. Instead, it's like a sex session that lasts too long due to whiskey dick—past the period of enjoyment and minus the period of climax. I discard of the cigarette into a nearby flower pot attached to the patio. The lack of satisfaction derived from the American Spirit is the closest I've felt to a being a woman since I wore my mother's heels around our townhome as a child. Pain, irritation, annoyance, and swindled by the allure of beauty.

I take my iPhone out from my back pocket and text Ernie, desperate for some level of intimacy existing outside the Royal Tree.

Me. What up, jive turkey?

Ernie. Not shit, cracka. Just watching Formula One races.

Ernie was the only black man I knew who was a fan of Indy car racing. I attribute it to his relationship with a German fräulein, Elsa, and her influence. They're yet to marry, despite having lived together for a few years, but I anticipate an engagement happening in the near future. If he ever musters up the gumption to make an honest woman out of her.

ME. You watching the Bravos later?

ERNIE. Yeah, man. You?

ME. Pho sho. Wanna watch wit me @ Royal Tree?

ERNIE. Yeah, I can do that? What time?

ME. Game's early—3:30 p.m. How bout you show at 3:00 p.m., and we kick it before opening pitch?

ERNIE. Works for me. See ya then.

ME. Cooool beans. See ya at 3:00 p.m.

I'll expect him later than 3:00 p.m. For all Ernie's positive attributes, his lack of punctuality when it comes to anything non–work related is one of his only shortcomings.

I put my phone down on a patio table outside and take another drink from my Guinness. *Might as well text Bob too*, I think to myself.

ME. Yo, what's up?

BOB. Just cleenin my apartment. U?

(Bob didn't text in Ebonics. He just couldn't spell for shit. Not even autocorrect could decipher his verbiage.)

ME. Hangin at Royal Tree.

BOB. Figers.

ME. You wanna come watch the Braves game later with Ernie and me?

BOB. Yeah, I can do that. Wut time?

ME. Game starts at 3:30 p.m. We were gonna meet at 3:00 p.m. Cool?

BOB. Yeah. I'll be there around 3:00 p.m.

ME. Niiiice. C ya then.

I holster my phone in my back pocket and take another drink from my beer. Soon, my oldest friends will arrive, and the gang will be back together. It has been a couple of weeks since we'd seen each other. And as much as I enjoyed Dane's company, I was eager to hang out with my longest-running comrades. Their company reminds me of better times, when the world was at our finger tips, as opposed to my reality of being in the palm of the world's hand.

I feel the sun beating down on my back. It's more soothing than uncomfortable. "Today is going to be a good day," I say out loud. Quietly. I'd better get back inside, near the AC, though, before the heat begins to irritate my eczema.

Back in the pub, I return to my seat next to Dane. He's onto another scotch and water. That's how long it takes to smoke an American Spirit. I'm still ahead of him on drinks, but he's gaining steam with the liquor. I'll hold off for now and stick to my beer but plan on dropping the hammer after the Braves game ends around dinnertime, once I've had time to get some more food in my belly to soak up the excess stout I've been consuming all afternoon.

I lean my elbows against the bar, perched, as if waiting for something to happen. Though little has unfolded thus far. Just the usual tit for tat with Dane and the constant stream of *SportsCenter* airings on ESPN. And then I hear the front door open. It's Les.

"Well, well, well, if it isn't the smoker's corner!" Les announces, strolling into the pub, his bald head shining in the sunlight reflecting from the windows and wearing gray sweat shorts and a UC Santa Cruz Banana Slugs t-shirt. He's an attorney during the week but dresses like an assistant college basketball coach on the weekends. He's a real down-to-earth fella, despite being the most successful patron of the Royal Tree by many, many salary dollars. And he loves to talk shit as much as I do—which I appreciate and which makes for entertaining banter.

"Hello, Les."

Dane and I greet each him with a handshake and a pat on each other's shoulders. Les takes a seat at the bar stool to my right, him and Dane completing the bookend with myself in the middle, riding bitch. It's a common seating arrangement for the three of us.

Les smiles cheerfully in my direction and gives me another pat on the shoulder. "How you doing?" he says in his New York accent.

"Not bad. You?"

"I have no complaints, Matthew. No complaints today."

Les is in high spirits today, as he tends to be most days, ever since beating colon cancer last winter. It was definitely a trying time for him, understandably. Les is Jewish and stereotypically tends to sway toward neuroticism, especially regarding his health. I'm sure he spiraled into thinking he might not make it through the year at some point, but he's a tough bastard and came out the other end with a positive attitude, which I find infectious. He's refreshed, rejuvenated, and eager to socialize with his bar buddies once again on this glorious summer day.

Tyler approaches us and addresses Les.

"How's it going Les?"

"It's going Tyler. How are you?"

"Just peachy. What can I get ya?"

"I'll have a vodka martini with blue cheese olives, please."

"Sure thing. Dirty?"

"Very."

"Flirting early today, I see."

"What? I just said I like it dirty."

"Mm-hmm. Be right back with your drink." Tyler walks away and mixes Les's martini.

Les swivels in his stool, back to facing Dane and me. "So, boys. You here to watch the game later or just holding court?"

"Watching the game. I need the Braves to lose so the Nationals can jump up in the division," says Dane.

I give Dane a surprised look. "Blasphemy!"

"What? I'm from DC. I'm a Nationals fan."

"Not today you aren't, Dane. This is Braves country, and if you want me to buy you a drink later, I'd better see your arm motioning some tomahawk chops today."

Dane laughs and responds, "I'll do my best to keep my DC fandom down to a minimum. How's that sound?"

"That's a start. Les, I'm guessing you're here for the game as well?"

"Well yeah! And while we're on the subject, go Mets!"

"Get outta here with that shit. I get the feeling you may be a problem later."

"You're damn right. Just wait till our Ace takes the mound. Then it'll be lights out."

"Yeah, lights out on his ass come the third inning after the Bravos hit some dingers off that motherfucker."

Tyler comes back carrying a martini and places it in front of Les.

"Thank you, Tyler."

"No problem!"

Les looks at Dane and me and raises his martini glass to toast. "Boys, to our health."

Dan and I raise our glasses in unison and air toast Les in solidarity. We each take long drinks from our glasses. Camaraderie at its best.

Les zeroes in on me and speaks so as only the two of us can hear. "So, Matt, how's the job hunt coming?"

"Eh, you know. Applying here and there. Mostly dead ends though."

"I'm sorry to hear that. You know, you're a bright guy. I'm sure something will come along eventually. Don't you have a degree?"

"Yeah, human resources."

"Well I'm sure there would be something you could find in that department. It's not like that's a nothing degree."

"You'd think, but every interview I go into gets shut down fairly quickly. I may have a degree, but with no experience in that field I'm kinda fucked."

"Well, how about this? You keep looking for another few weeks. See if any of these interviews materialize. And if nothing pops up, I'll see about getting you an entry-level job at my firm."

"Really? That'd be great, Les. I'd really appreciate that."

"Sure. But look, it may not be in HR. I'd just have to see what is available. Could be something in the mailroom or as an aid or whatever. But I mean, who knows? You come on, do well, maybe take some law classes at night or online, and eventually we could get you on as a paralegal."

"That would be amazing. I'd definitely be interested in that. Even for the opportunity. You know, I was prelaw at one point in college, so I got some business law classes under my belt already."

"That's a start."

"Would these jobs be hourly or are we talking salary?"

"Ha ha. Let's not get too ahead of ourselves here, okay. I still have to see if there's even something available for you."

"Just saying, a salary would be nice. I've had issues in the past with hourly jobs. I've found there tend to be some clerical errors that arise, and a set salary would clear up a lot of those problems."

"Just keep looking for work. And if you can't find anything, I'll see if there's a place for you at the firm. Deal?"

"Deal."

I cheer Les for his generosity and finish off my beer with a long gulp. Only leaving the frothy foam at the bottom of the glass. Cold spit. No use for that anymore. I may be a law man soon. I knew it was going to be a good day.

9

I step outside the Royal Tree again onto the front patio. It's time for another smoke break. I take out my last American Spirit and light up. I suffer through another "all-natural tobacco" cigarette, and all I want now is to work my way down to the filter as quickly as possible. It's an unrealistic goal at the rate the cherry amber is burning. But I progress, damned to suffer, like Sisyphus being punished by rolling a boulder uphill for an eternity in Hades.

I check my watch. It's 2:05 p.m. The day is moving by slowly. That's how I prefer it on the weekends. Hopefully it feels like a long one. Few things are as unsatisfying as a weekend that passes by too quickly. A couple of blinks, and it's over. Then it's Monday and time to wake up to go to work. However, I'm still out of work, despite Les's offer to help, so every day is a weekend for me. I'll have to enjoy this period of unemployment while it lasts. As long as the unemployment checks keep rolling in.

I look up at the sun, blocking the rays with my hand, letting the light hit my face, taking in my vitamins for the day. As I stare at the flaming star, its warmth provides me with a sense of peace and assurance, much due to the possibility of gainful employment in the near future. *Soon I'll be in an office.* Finally, I'll put those four years of college courses to use. I had given up hope some years back. After the first eighteen months to two years of failed job interview after failed job interview, it became hard to imagine ever putting on a collared shirt for work. It's not that I desired an office job; it's that I desire an office job's salary.

Working outdoors suits me best, but the pay is shit, and the constant sweating only makes the eczema worsen. I feel that the stress relief of a salary would allow me the ability to pay the bills, afford health insurance to visit a dermatologist for the rashes, and even take a lady out on a proper date that didn't involve meeting at a dive bar or for slices of pizza from a bodega. In the meantime, I'll just drink cheap beer and liquor and scratch the eczema itches away.

The itches return, and I resume grazing my left foot over the location of the rashes residing under my pant leg. Goddamn selvedge denim jeans are a truly unforgiving fabric to rub against open sores. I feel my jeans dampen on the inside of my pant leg from the eczema sores oozing and bleeding. Ugh, I fucking hate damp denim. Wet socks may be worse, but for now, damp denim takes the cake.

I stop scratching and return to smoking the American Spirit, now halfway burnt down to the butt. When there's only a filter remaining, I'll head back inside and order another beer. Maybe a Coors Light. It's a warm day and an ice-cold silver bullet would taste amazing right now. It also helps that it's the drink special for the day—three-dollar longnecks. I'll take it.

A feeling of loneliness creeps over me outside on the patio, and I decide to make some form of human contact with the rest of the world. So I take out my phone and scroll through my contacts for someone to text. I reach "Holly Royal Tree"—the cute blonde from the night before. Might as well see what she's up to. I've never been a farmer, but I suspect I can still plant a seed here and there.

Me. Hey there. It's Matt from the bar last night. How's it going?

I suck at the cigarette, and after a few more puffs, finally I reach the filter and flick it into the street. Another fantastic twirl of a smoking dog end moves through the air. Marvelous to watch. *I'm getting a knack for the dramatics*, I compliment myself. I check my phone again. No response. About what I expected. I return to my stool inside the bar.

I order a Coors Light from Tyler and check my phone. No new messages. Tyler returns less than a minute later with the Coors Light—the mountains on the label a solid blue color. It's good and cold. I take a sip from the bottle and relish the chilled taste, masking the watered-down flavor. It tastes just like the first beer I stole from my father's refrigerator when I was ten years old. Nostalgia kicks in. For a brief moment, I feel like I'm young again and in my parent's backyard, climbing trees and shooting BB guns at empty Coke cans and action figures. What a time that was. Too bad I can't go back. Only in my mind's eye. But that's what memories are for. I take another sip of nostalgia.

Fifteen minutes later, my phone vibrates. There's a text alert from Holly Royal Tree. She responded. I feel a rush of excitement overcome my senses in anticipation of reading her response.

HOLLY. Hi there. I'm good. How are you?

She's engaging the conversation. Better not screw this up. Think of a good response.

ME. I'm doing great. Just hanging out with some friends, waiting to watch the Braves game. You?

HOLLY. Well that sounds fun. GO BRAVOS! I'm just hanging out with my sister at PCM having drinks on the rooftop. It's such a nice day out.

She calls them the Bravos. Only a true fan would refer to them that way. This interaction could turn into something worthwhile. And also, what the fuck is PCM?

ME. Yeah, go Bravos! I hope they win. I'm not quite sure what PCM is, but it sounds like fun. Are y'all up to anything tonight?

HOLLY. Ha. It's Ponce City Market. Down in midtown. Have you never been?

She didn't answer my question about what her plans are for tonight. Maybe she's avoiding it.

Me. Oh ha. Nah I've never made it down there. I don't venture into midtown too often. Mostly stay out in Dunwoody, or I'll go to East Atlanta.

Holly. Wow, that's surprising you've never been to Ponce City. It has some cool shops and restaurants. This is actually my first time on the rooftop. East Atlanta is pretty cool. I go to the Earl with my sister every once in a while.

Me. Yeah, I like the Earl. Fun spot. Are you hanging out at PCM the rest of the day?

Holly. Yeah. It's fun, as long as you don't mind smelling like a cigarette at the end of the night. Ha … I'm not sure yet. Probably will be here for a little while longer though. Are you just watching the Bravos game with your friends tonight?

She asked about my plans for the night. She's interested in what I have going on later.

Me. Cool. I was planning on watching the game this afternoon but don't have any set plans for after. Do you think you'll be doing anything later on tonight?

Holly. I don't have any real plans for later tonight. Maybe just hanging out watching TV or something.

Me: well, if you're free later, would you wanna meet me at Royal Tree after the Braves game is over? Say around 8:00 p.m.?

Holly doesn't respond immediately. She's taking a few minutes. My guess is she's consulting on this with her sister. Hopefully her sister doesn't mind sharing her time with Holly for the evening. A couple more minutes go by. No response. Shit, this may not happen after all. Another minute later, my phone vibrates. It's an iMessage from Holly Royal Tree.

Holly. Ha you wanna meet at the same bar we were last night?

Me. Ha, well I was gonna watch the game here anyways and figured it might be fitting. Familiar territory and everything. Ja.

HOLLY. Ha. Okay. I guess that'd be fine. Yeah, I can meet you there at 8:00 p.m.

Success. She's in. The euphoria is pouring over me, running from my head to my feet. I don't even notice the nagging eczema pain any more. All I can feel is the elation of having secured a date with this fine, golden creature. I take a sip from my Coors Light and briefly rejoice, before returning to the text thread.

ME. Awesome. Sounds good. I'll see ya at 8:00 p.m. then.

HOLLY: Alrighty, see you later!

The date is officially on the books. Victory. I'll see her tonight. I check my watch again—2:40 p.m. I have over five hours before she arrives. Plenty of time to have some celebratory drinks before I have to sober up for the date. I figure a few more hours of good solid drinking, and then an hour to ninety minutes of water and coffee to regain my wits. I've never been great with math, but this should be a simple enough equation to solve.

"Tyler!"

"Yeah?"

"Could I get a Bulleit Bourbon on the rocks?"

"Sure. You want a single or a double?"

I may no longer be single if this date pans out the way I hope it will. "Let's make it a double."

Tyler pours out my glass of bourbon and delivers it to me in less than a minute, with a coaster underneath. A glass of liquor with ice can cause the glass to condensate and ruin the wood bar top with wet ring stains on the finish. I lift the glass to my lips and take a sip of the bourbon. I enjoy the burning sensation running down my throat, because it feels as if the drink is performing its job efficiently. The top shelf Bulleit bourbon tastes smooth on my tongue, and for the duration of the drink, I will be in a higher class than the one I currently occupy. For I, now have multiple prospects. In work and in love.

10

It's 2:45 p.m. I'm waiting at the bar for Ernie and Bob to arrive. Still working on my double Bulleit Bourbon on the rocks. I try not to slam these too quickly for a couple of reasons: (1) I enjoy the taste and wish for it to last as long as possible before the ice melts and dilutes the drink, and (2) I don't have a ton of money to spend today. Unemployment from the state only pays $335 a week, in addition to what I get from the federal government. Not bad government assistance, but rent prices have skyrocketed the last few years and I need to conserve just enough to keep a roof over my head.

Today, however, I'm not an unemployed manual labor grunt with no female prospects. On the contrary. I'm now a legal firm prospect with a lady on the way. I'll put the tab on the credit card. We'll settle up at closing. For now, I celebrate with my friends.

Some more bar patrons roll in, presumably to watch the game. The pub is about half full now, having amassed a whopping twenty to twenty-five people. Among them are some usual suspects. I can't recall their names for the most part—only their faces and their behaviors after one too many.

The one I do notice is Baby Baby. An older man, roughly fifty-five, though he looks seventy-five due to decades of chronic alcohol abuse, he's a chimer. He can't help but interject himself in private conversations with mindless anecdotes; conspiracy theories; and bullshit, misguided bravado. Not to mention his proclivity for using innuendo and making sexual advances in his remarks toward the bartenders—mainly Tyler. I'm not a fan, and neither are Les and Dane. I'll admit, though, Baby Baby is quite charming on occasion, when he's not coming across too forward or inserting himself in situations that don't warrant his appearance. Still yet, he's earned an uncomfortable laugh from me here and there—mostly due to the realization of the absurdity of his ego and mind alike.

This afternoon, I can see him rubbernecking his way into Dane, Les, and my direction. We try not to notice him, which is easier said than done, given his hands tremble from the booze shakes, causing the ice in his glasses to clink and clank together like a maraca.

Les leans in and asks Dane and I about betting on the game. "You boys putting any money on the ball game?"

Dane quickly replies, "Oh no, not me. I've learned my lesson in the past. Ha ha."

"Matt, how about you?"

"Eh, shit I don't know, Les. What did you have in mind?"

"Well, you see, I got a wager going with a bookie on this one. No point spread. I'm taking the Mets to win, plus I have a side bet on the under for the game."

"Which is?"

"Six runs. All I need is five or less and the Mets to pull it out."

"I know how the bets work. And the only thing the Mets are gonna pull out is their asses when the Braves show them to the crowd during this upcoming spanking."

Dane laughs boisterously.

Les is amused but fires back. "Yeah, well, we'll see, wiseass. I'll tell you what. We can do a bet just between us."

"I'm in. How you wanna play it?"

"We can bet it straight up. You take Atlanta, you win. I take New York, I win."

"I can do that. How much?"

"Twenty bucks?"

"You got a goddamn deal, Lesley."

This isn't a great move on my part, seeing as I'm living on un-employment. But it's a gamble. I'll just look at betting with a little cash on hand—$25 as another side bet with the landlords and bill collectors. Regardless, Les and I shake hands.

Let's make it interesting. I turn to Dane. "Dane, you sure you don't want in on this?"

"No. You two go ahead. I don't have enough confidence in either of these teams right now."

"Ye of little faith."

Baby Baby leans farther in to address our group, speaking in a southern Louisiana drawl. "You boys got a little money up on this here coming game?"

"Yeah, only a few bucks," Les replies.

"I don't know how you boys here bet on them baseball games. You know all those games are fixed, right? Like betting on cham-pionship wrestling. Listen, baby, I tell ya, they already know who's gonna win before the contest even begins."

Les shakes his head dismissively and turns his chair in Baby Baby's direction, ready to address the court. "Oh, come on, Baby Baby! You know that isn't true. My god. It's not like Pete Rose is still in the league."

"You think there ain't no other fellas like him doing the same thing? Damn boy, I swear, you can't be that I."

"Baby Baby, not everything is some kind of conspiracy. And even if the game were fixed, it's not like we know that anyhow. So therefore, we'd still be betting on an outcome that neither of us is aware of."

"You can go on ahead and use your fancy lawyer reasoning on someone else. I'm just saying y'all are playing a fool's game here."

"You know what, Baby Baby, just go on back to your vodka sweet tea and let us have our fun, all right?"

"Fine, baby! Fine! Y'all don't want my help, I won't offer it up again any which way!"

"Thank you. Have a good afternoon." Les finishes his closing argument and swivels back toward Dane and I.

We can't stop grinning over his interaction with Baby Baby and the differences in their accents waging a verbal battle. Les v. Louisiana Board of Noneducation.

"Have a good talk, Les?" Dane asks sarcastically.

Les shakes his head and plants his palm on his face.

Then again, back toward the end of the bar and Baby Baby's direction, we hear him pipe up once more. This time his drawl is aimed at Tyler. "Tyler, baby. Can you pour me a John Daly?" asks Baby Baby. (A John Daly is an Arnold Palmer but with vodka.)

"You betcha, Baby Baby." Tyler responds, taking his empty glass behind the bar to mix another cocktail.

Tyler mixes the John Daly and puts it in front of Baby Baby on the bar top, coaster underneath.

"Thank ya, baby. And if you could, I'm gonna need some extra sugar with this here drink."

"Sure." Tyler hands Baby Baby six packets of cane sugar. "Here's some sugar packets for ya."

"Thank ya, baby. And maybe later, when ya get off, I can take ya out for a nightcap. Ya just gotta make sure to bring some sugar with ya." Baby Baby flirts with Tyler, winking as he finishes his proposal.

"Ha, well I don't know about that one. My boyfriend might not like that too much."

"Don't worry about him. He can stay in the car and give you a ride home after. Ha!"

"Whatever you say, Baby Baby." Tyler says, brushing off his advances and chalking it up to him being another dirty old man.

Dane, Les, and I return our focus back toward each other and shake our heads at Baby Baby again. Inappropriate remarks don't bother us for the most part, but Tyler is like a close friend or a sister to the regulars. And knowing this is most likely the first of a number of additional unwanted advances she'll receive today from Baby Baby only makes our skin crawl the more.

"My god. He's such a schmuck. Acting like this is Shoeless Joe Jackson and the Chicago Black Sox taking the field today. And that shit he says to Tyler just pisses me off even more," Les complains.

"Christ, she's young enough to be his daughter," Dane says.

"Fucking asshole." Les reiterates his opinion on Baby Baby.

We each take more sips of drinks as I continue waiting for Bob and Ernie to arrive. Shouldn't be long now. I've known Bob and Ernie for a very long time—twenty years to be exact—and I can tell roughly what time they'll show. Ernie will be late, at least by fifteen minutes. Bob, however, should appear any minute. He's an early bird. I check my watch—2:55 p.m. I look out the front window of the Royal Tree, and there he is, as predicted.

Bob opens the front door of the Royal Tree. He's a tall, burly man, resembling an ex-football player or pro wrestler. A true jock type, but with a limited understanding of sports and instead possessing an encyclopedic knowledge of pop culture, books, film, and music.

Bob has a degree in public relations and works as a used car salesman at a dealership in another suburb of Atlanta. He seems to be doing well for himself in his career, pulling in a decent salary plus commission and a company car. Recently, he purchased his first home not too far from where we grew up as kids. One could say his success in sales is attributed to his large presence and being blessed with the gift of gab. Whatever it is, he's made it work for him.

His broad shoulders fill the doorway as he enters the pub. He's dressed in familiar attire for him—cargo shorts, Queens of the Stone Age t-shirt, and New Balance sneakers.

I stand to meet him at the bar. "Well if it isn't Mr. Bobert. What's up?"

"Just being awesome, man. You been here long?"

"Nah, not that long."

"Bullshit. I know you've been here since they opened."

"Ha, possibly."

"You goddamn degenerate. I know you too well. You're like Jim Morrison or Janis Joplin but without the talent and all the booze, ha ha."

"Fuck off. Wanna take a seat?"

"Yeah, where? At the bar?"

"Yes, sir. Dane and Les are here too."

Bob walks toward Dane and Les at the bar and shakes their hands. Les and Dane say their hellos.

"Hey there, Bob. How are you, man?"

"Good, Dane. How are you?"

"Great! Just hanging out. Waiting for the game to start."

"Yeah, I'm here to watch the game also with this lowlife over here." Bob gestures in my direction.

I throw up a peace sign in return. Les stands from his seat.

"Looks like the gang is starting to show up. Howya doin', Bob?"

"Great, Les. How are you?"

"I'm doing just fine, young sir. Here. You wanna take my seat?"

"I don't wanna put you out."

"No, no. No worries. I can move to the seat on the other side of Dane. I'll let you two gents sit together."

"Thanks! I appreciate it."

"Absolutely."

Les grabs his martini and reseats himself to the left of Dane, allowing Bob to plop down on Les' old stool.

Tyler moseys down the back of the bar toward Bob to take his order. "Hi there!"

"Hi!"

"Watcha havin'?"

"Umm, I'll have a vodka soda, please."

"Sure. Any preference in vodka?"

"No. Well is fine."

"Kay. Single or a double?"

"I'm driving later, so I'll just have a single."

"Alrighty. BRB."

Tyler turns away from us, pours Bob his cocktail, and slides it toward him.

Bob takes his opening sip of the vodka soda. "Ahh, goddamn, that's good. You know, there's not much difference between cheap vodka and the expensive stuff, right?"

"I've heard something like that before. You can taste the difference if you drink it straight though." Matt adds.

"Maybe, but when it's chilled with a mixer, you can barely tell the difference. Half the price for essentially the same taste."

"You going with the more-bang-for-your-buck philosophy?"

"Always."

Bob takes another drink from his cocktail. This time, it's a smaller sip than a swig. He's driving, so he won't drink too much. The last time he drank too much here, he left his car and took an Uber home—only to return to find his car window bashed out and a bag containing sweaty workout clothes missing from the back seat. Not a huge loss for him but a pain in the ass nonetheless.

"So, what'd you get into last night?" Bob inquires.

"Not shit. Just hung out here."

"Of course you did. Do you think you spend more time here than the staff?"

"Ha, possibly. They only work single and double shifts. Me? I open and close."

"I know you do, Billy Ray."

"What about you? You do anything last night?"

"I had a date."

"How'd that go?"

"Wanna smell my fingers?"

"Ha. Nah, I don't wanna whiff of any of those lot lizards you pick up off the highway."

"Ha, fuck off. No lot lizard here, bro. This chick was prime."

"Oh yeah?"

"Bigly. She had the looks of a *Scream*-era Neve Campbell type but with those crazy Manson Family member eyes. Hot doggie! It was intense."

"I bet. Glad you had a good time."

Bob always had a story regarding his sex-capades. He fancied himself a "cocksman" and backed it up for the most part. If you asked him his "number," you'd most assuredly get one in the fifties or sixties. Not bad for a thirty-one-year-old. I believe, though, he's more of a quantity versus a quality man. Not to say he didn't have some gems under his belt, but he'd had an equal numbers of subpar level women, as far as conventional attractiveness and looks go. My numbers are lower, but I'm a bit choosier. I don't get on my back for just any cowgirl looking for a ride. I need wining and dining—or at least a few drinks in me before I'll consider performing. This is likely a product of having grown up surrounded by women, primarily.

Bob was the opposite of me in that sense—an only child and more self-centric. It's the duality of our friendship that has sustained us, kept us both interested throughout the years. Whereas I'm more of a man of chance encounter and circumstance, he is a true hunter. Once he lasered in on a potential receiver of his masculinity, he rarely went home defeated. His women were more than up for it too. Something about a large, stocky man put them at ease—like they were safe with him. And that made them more willing to allow him to conquer them.

Bob took full advantage of his stature. And he had charisma to back it up. He was notoriously great at first impressions, leading to many a one-night stand. Few return customers though. He wasn't a relationship man. "Couldn't be tied down," he'd tell me. Could be his breed? Could be a fear of commitment? No matter. I am no judge when it comes to animalistic instinct.

We are all animals. We're born. We nurse. We grow up. We eat. We shit. We sleep. We screw. We live. And we die. There's not much mystery. It's the in between that defines us. And Bob's in between revolves around sexual conquests. Simple enough.

Bob and I continue to sit at the bar chatting, discussing day to day minutia, while Dane and Les hang back, lost in their own conversation, affording Bob and me time to catch up. I have another pull from my glass of bourbon. It's time to tell Bob about the Holly encounter the night before.

"I met a girl last night."

"You mean a guy?"

"No wiseass, a real girl. Cute too."

"Where? Here?"

"Yeah."

"I didn't think hot chicks came to the Royal Tree?"

"You'd be surprised."

"So, what happened? Was she just here hanging out?"

"Sort of. She was here for a postwork happy hour thing. She's a nurse and came in with a gaggle of other nurses after their shifts ended."

"A nurse? Wow. Nice. I've always wanted to fuck a nurse."

"Why?"

"They just seem like they can take care of you, ya know? Familiar with the human anatomy. Know all the right buttons to push. I get it."

"Well not all nurses work in proctology. So, in your case, you might be outta luck."

"Fuck off. So, did y'all hook up or what?"

"Nah, man. Just talked. I got her number though. Texted her before you got here. We're supposed to meet up later after the game."

"So, what you're saying is we're not bro-ing down later?"

"Ha. Sorry not tonight. We got all afternoon though. I'm not supposed to meet her for another five hours—around 8:00 p.m."

"Okay, that's cool. I'll just go fuck myself then."

"Ha, whatever. It's not like you haven't bailed before to meet up with some dame."

"I know. I'm just bustin' your balls. Well, good luck tonight."

"Thanks."

"Where are you meeting her?"

"Here."

"Here? Didn't you just say y'all hung out here yesterday?"

"Ha, yeah. But I told her I already had plans with you and Ernie today to watch the Braves here and that she could just pop on over afterward. I figured I'd already be at the pub, and it was a place we both knew. Plus, if I remember correctly, I don't think she lives too far away either."

"I don't know, man. Sounds like a weird move. She's gonna think you're some sort of barfly."

"Ha, well she wouldn't be too off base."

"Yeah, but I'd just think you wouldn't want her to get that impression of you. At least not upfront."

"Well, we'll see what happens. She didn't seem too weirded out by it based on her texts. Like, I said, I think she knows I live close by, and I'm meeting friends here. So, it's not like I'm coming across as some sad loner—"

"Which you are."

"Ha. But it's not gonna seem odd because I'm hanging out with other people. Plus, it's Saturday. Everyone kicks it at the bars on the weekends. So, who gives a shit?"

"I understand your logic, but I would've just suggested another location."

"It's not a serious date at the moment. We're just meeting up for drinks. Real casual. Still feeling each other out. If all goes well, then I'll look into making a dinner reservation. Until then, c'est la vie.

"All right. You do you, I guess."

We both take a break from our banter to enjoy more swigs of liquor. I'm definitely feeling a buzz now but not drunk yet. If I can manage to stick to light beers and an occasional coffee or water throughout the duration of the ball game, I should be good and lubricated yet still charming and sharp for my rendezvous with Holly tonight. The key is remaining loose enough to accentuate confidence but not drunk enough to seem sloppy or obnoxious. I can save that for when I get home.

Bob continues to show his interest in my upcoming date and resumes questioning me on the details. I'm happy to oblige. Just one more drink of bourbon first.

"So, what does she look like? Got a pic?"

"No, man, I don't have a pic. We just met. I don't even know her last name."

"Fair enough, but what does she look like though?"

"Blonde, curly hair. Brown eyes. Probably mid-twenties. Maybe five-five, five-six. Like I said, real pretty."

"Sounds promising. Who does she look like? Like, which celebrity?"

"Hmmm … I'd say kinda like a young Julia Roberts or Kyra Sedgwick—almost like a blonder, *Pretty Woman*-era Julia Roberts to be more exact."

"Wow."

"Yeah, she's smart too. I mean, I figure you have to be if you're a nurse. Lot of schooling. That's why I'm having to bail on hanging out after the game. I see potential."

"Oh yeah, I get it. I'd do the same thing, mijo."

"Oh, I know you would, muchacho."

We return to our drinks. Bob, slowly sipping at the vodka soda, now half empty. Me, polishing off the last of the Bulleit Bourbon. I drain the last drops from the bottom of the glass and take a few half-melted ice cubes in my mouth, tossing the cubes from side to side with my tongue before crushing them with my molars.

Tyler witnesses me finish my drink and approaches. "Another?"

"Uh, nah, but I think I'll switch back to Coors Light."

"You really like to change up your orders on us, don't ya?"

"I just like to keep you and my body guessing."

"Mission accomplished. I never know what you're gonna order next. Ha."

Tyler walks toward the refrigerator and pulls out a Coors Light. Mountains blue. Twists the cap off and passes it to me. I pick up the beer, take a swig of the chilled beverage, and rest it on a coaster.

Bob is on his phone. I can see he's opened a dating app and is swiping on women he finds attractive. He quickly glances at each profile pic and makes hasty judgments on which females interest him. Physically. He never reads the bios.

"You looking for potential mates?"

"Always, mijo. Always."

"You get any matches today?"

"Not yet, but it's still early."

"What's wrong with that one?" I say, pointing out an attractive brunette he just swiped nay on.

"I can tell she doesn't look like her pictures."

"How so?"

"The angle her camera was at when she took it. You gotta be skeptical of any image taken from above. It hides the double chin and gives the illusion of thinness."

"I haven't known you to pass on some action just because they were heavyset in the past."

"If they were in front of me in person, I wouldn't turn them down. But if I'm cherry-picking, I consistently pick a more petite broad."

Bob continues swiping left and right on dating profiles, while I check my watch. It's 3:15 p.m. The game is about to start. Ernie should be here by now. I'll give him till 3:30 p.m. before I'll call. In the meantime, I'll ask Tyler to turn the TV behind the bar to the Braves-Mets game.

"Tyler?"

"Yeah?" she hollers from the other side of the bar.

"Can you please turn the TV to Fox Sports? The Braves are about to come on."

"And the Mets!" Les chimes in unexpectedly.

"Fuck the Mets!" I yell in return.

The other bar patrons laugh and cheer at my insult of the New York ball club. Tyler finishes serving drinks to another group of customers before grabbing the remote control and turning the channel to Fox Sports. It's pregame, but the broadcasters are already giving their assessments of the two teams and what we may expect from the starting pitchers this afternoon.

Not long after tuning in to the pregame show, Baby Baby offers up his two cents. "The fix is in, boys!"

"Pipe down, Baby Baby, and just enjoy the game." Les replies.

It's apparent Les is still irritated with Baby Baby's assessment. I can't blame him. Baby Baby leans back on his stool and takes another drink of his John Daly. The ice in the glass vibrates as his handshakes. Something tells me he won't keep his mouth shut for too long.

12

It's now 3:25 p.m., and Ernie's still yet to be seen. The Braves and Mets have taken the field. The Mets' starting pitcher—their ace—is on the mound. He's throwing warm-up pitches to his catcher. I have to give it to New York's ace. The guy has a cannon for an arm to go along with his long golden locks. "Thor-looking motherfucker," I mutter to myself. He'll be a tough match for the Braves' batters today. Fox Sports brings up a graphic on the screen showing the pitcher's stats for the year. Sub 2.00 ERA for the season thus far. Shit. It's at this point I'm realizing the bet I made with Les may have been a mistake. Luckily, I have enough cash on me to cover my ass in case Atlanta can't pull off the win. After all, it's only twenty dollars. But it's twenty dollars I can't afford to lose at this juncture in my life. Not until I find another job or Les comes through with something at the firm.

I take a drink from my beer and watch the TV behind the bar. The Mets' pitcher has finished warming up as the Braves' batting order is announced. Pretty solid from top to bottom. A good collection of seasoned veterans and young talent balance each other out quite nicely. The Braves are leading their division up to this point in the season, holding a 4.5 game lead over the second-place team in the NL East. The lineup has been effective, and this reassures my hope of winning the bet, putting little to no dent in Les's pocket, and making me twenty dollars richer. Anything helps. Despite leading in the NL East, the Braves are far from the best team in the league overall. Los Angeles and Houston have a slight edge on them. A mix of crafty veterans with deep pockets and savvy managers will do that.

Even though the Bravos are not the most dominant team in the league, they're easily the most handsome. Any number of their infielders could qualify for matinee idols, soiling the panties of any number of female fans, or male fans for that matter. The TV camera zooms in on the Braves' leadoff man taking practice swings before heading to the plate. You can almost hear the women slipping out of their seats as he struts into the batter's box.

Bob swivels his head away from the TV toward the door, like a dog perking up when it hears someone approaching the front door.

"Ernie's here."

"Where?"

I turn my head toward the entrance, viewing Ernie reaching the patio, just on the opposite side of the glass front door—3:29 p.m. He arrives just it in time for the first pitch. Happy to see he could make it.

Ernie opens the front door and walks into the pub, waving hello to us on his way to the bar. Ernie is an unusually tall man, about six foot six, and is often asked if he's an NBA player. To this, he often replies, "Not every tall black man plays basketball." But he could've. Always a great athlete in his youth, he chose to focus on school instead of athletics in college and earned a master's degree in finance. He was always efficient and calculated with numbers and wise with money. The guy knew how to stretch a dollar better than anyone I'd ever known but without being cheap. Not an easy task.

Ernie was able to parlay his education and his financial aptitude into a career as a day trader—working with local companies on how best to invest their pension funds and 401(k)s. In addition to his business ventures, he had also made himself a few bucks playing the stock market while in college, investing a percentage of his paychecks from his first jobs out of high school in mutual funds and Apple and Uber stock. Apple already had a long-established presence in the market, but it was his early investments in Uber that really made him some money—enough to pay his college tuition and purchase a new Lexus after graduation. I wish I had made a similar move back in those days. Instead, I chose to invest my money in concert tickets, bar tabs, and the occasional pair of jeans. Whatever. I had a good time. I'll consider the memories as a return on my investments.

Ernie, now inside the bar, is well dressed. He's wearing a pair of khaki pants, dry fit golf polo, and brown leather Adidas shoes—an upscale outfit for a Saturday outing in a bar. *Always business casual, this guy*, I think, taking another sip of beer.

Before Ernie greets Bob and me, he shakes hands with Dane and Les. Paying his respects to the elder statesmen.

"How's it going, guys?"

"Great, Ernie. How are things with you?" says Les.

"Pretty good, just got done playing a round of golf, and now I'm up here to meet those two assholes to watch the Braves," replies Ernie, pointing at Bob and me.

"Ha ha, I figured. Glad to see the whole gang is together today."

"Yeah, should be fun. Dane, how's life?"

"Going well, Ernie. How about you?" answers Dane.

"No complaints. Just hoping the Braves can pull further ahead in the division." Ernie notices Dane's Washington Nationals cap and calls him out. "Oh, man, you might need to take that hat off in this city. Someone might kill you," Ernie jokes with Dane.

"Ha ha. Never! I'd be happy to die a Nationals fan!"

"Ha. I like the team spirit. Well, I'm gonna go see what those clowns over there are up to."

Ernie, Dane, and Les shake hands once again. Ernie steps around them and makes his way to our stool area of the bar. Bob and

I both rise from our seats and embrace Ernie with brief handshakes and familiar hugs, followed by pats on the back. It's apparent to any onlookers that the three of us have a long history.

"How's it going?" asks Ernie.

"Decent. You made it just in time for the first pitch," I inform him.

The opening pitch is tossed out by Thor. Take one and a strike. The Braves' initial handsome leadoff man is in the hole to start. Good eye though. No need to swing at the first pitch. Let's see what else Thor has in his arsenal.

Ernie takes a seat in the stool to the right of Bob. Ernie and I now have him flanked. This seating arrangement works best for us. Bob has a knack for steering the conversation into territories that make it easier to keep the banter afloat.

Tyler approaches the three of us and asks for our drink orders. "Howdy! So, what can I get ya?" she asks Ernie.

"Hi! I'll take whatever IPA you got on tap," Ernie orders.

"Sounds good. Basement IPA work?"

"Yeah that's fine."

"Cool. And are you two okay with drinks for now?"

"I'll do another vodka soda," Bob says.

"And I'll have another Coors Light," I add to the order, before sucking down the last swallow of beer from the bottle.

"Alrighty. Be right back with those drinks."

Tyler leaves us for the moment to retrieve our booze for the first inning.

"What are you all dressed up for?" I ask Ernie.

"Just got done playing golf," Ernie responds.

"With who?"

"My dad."

"How's he doing?"

"Good, man. Retired. Living the dream. All that stuff."

"Glad he's enjoying retirement. I've been enjoying a temporary retirement myself. Haven't picked up golf yet though."

"Ha. Oh, is that what you're calling it? Don't worry. I'm sure you'll find your way to the green eventually."

"I always figured Matt for more of a Putt-Putt man," Bob chimes in.

We laugh in unison. Bob frequently finds a way to draw amusement out of my misfortune. It's part of the dynamic. No matter. I can take it.

"How's the job hunt going, by the way?" asks Ernie.

"It's going. May have a lead on an office job. Could be getting out of this heat, once and for all. Swinging a sledgehammer may soon be a thing of the past. Ain't that right, Les?"

"Do what?" asks Les, confusedly.

"Yeah that's right. Les knows."

"I know the top of the Braves' lineup isn't looking too good, right now." Les reminds us of the state of the game.

The Braves now have two outs and the third batter is down two strikes with three balls. Full count. Thor lets rip a fastball on the inside corner. Strike three. Out. End of the first half of the inning.

"Fuck!" I yell.

"Ha ha. Gonna be a long day, Matt." Les laughs.

"It's still early, counselor. Just keep my twenty dollars crisp."

Tyler returns with two beers and a vodka soda. She places them in front of us with coasters underneath to respect the mahogany counter top. We each pick up our drinks and cheers.

"Boys, here's to the day off. Or as Matt refers to it, any other day," Bob toasts, mockingly.

We clink our drinks and take a gulp. Refreshing. Almost makes me forget about the Bravos' slow start.

"Well, we can't all sell lemons on wheels."

"Hey, asshole, I don't sell lemons. I sell quality pre-owned automobiles," Bob answers.

"Yeah, I bet the Better Business Bureau would be interested to hear about the odometers you've rolled back on them as well."

"Listen, what I do with my inventory is between me and God. And if you keep your mouth shut, there could be a '97 Ford Ranger in your future. For the right price, of course."

"I'd rather Flintstone my ass about town. But thanks for the offer."

"Just let me know. I think you'd look really classy in something for say, $500, $600."

"I'll have to get back to you on that. Once I've had time to prepare to haggle."

"You cheap fuck."

We laugh again and take more sips of our drinks. The top of the Mets' batting order is up to the plate. Down go the first two batters. The Braves walk the three-hole hitter, and now it's the cleanup man's turn. He takes the first two pitches looking. Strikes. The Braves' starting pitcher throws out a couple of breaking balls out of the strike zone. It's a two-two count. Then comes a changeup. The Mets' cleanup man swings and misses. Strike three. End of the inning. Still a 0–0 game. I happily take another swig of my beer. The mountains are still blue. Let's hope they remain that way.

13

Ernie, Bob, and I are watching the game. The score remains 0–0 at the end of the second inning, and now seems like a great time to step outside for a smoke break. Even though I'm out of cigarettes. Not to worry. Ernie has informed Bob and me he's brought his weed vape pen with him to the pub. It's an easy and less expensive way to have a good time than what alcohol will allow. Ernie remains financially efficient.

We step outside onto the patio before Ernie removes the vape pen from his khaki pocket. Ernie takes the first hit and exhales a cloud of smoke that results in Bob and me becoming fidgety as we wait for our turn at bat. I can feel my eczema start to itch again as I wait for Ernie to finish his puff.

"Is this an indica or sativa?" I ask Ernie as he passes me the vape pen.

"It's an upper. Straight sativa."

"Groovy."

I take a drag from the pen, inhaling the vapor into my lungs and holding it for a few counts before exhaling the faux smoke into the summer air. A slight cough emerges from my chest and out my mouth as the herb infiltrates my body.

"You good?" Ernie asks, laughingly.

"I'm golden, pony boy. Golden."

My eczema irritations subside moments after the initial intake of sativa. More mother nature's natural medicine than reefer madness. I hand the pen to Bob, and he takes failed hits from the device, struggling to successfully generate a solid intake of the sativa.

"What the fuck? It doesn't feel like I'm getting a good hit," Bob announces in frustration.

"Here, hold the button down while you inhale," Ernie says didactically.

"Yeah, quit being such an amateur. Hold the button and suck like you need the money," I interrupt.

After a couple more attempts, Bob learns his way around the vape pen and withdraws a quality hit. He holds it in and exhales after telling me to "fuck off." I like his spirit.

Bob hands the pen back to its owner, and Ernie hits it again before passing it back to me.

Never one to look a gift horse in the mouth, I oblige and return to the pen.

"You hear Matt's got a date later?" says Bob.

"Really? With who? Anyone we know?" asks Ernie.

"Some chick he met up here last night."

I finish my second hit from the weed pen and pass it to Bob. He takes a deep inhale and passes it back to Ernie. He holsters the pen in the front of his khakis before we can take even more pulls from the mouthpiece, draining the remnants of cannabis oil from the cartridge.

"For real? Way to go, Matty Light," Ernie congratulates.

"Ha, thanks. Yeah, I'm meeting her up here after the game ends."

"What's her name?" asks Ernie.

"Holly."

"Holly what? She from around here?"

"I don't know, man. Just met her. She apparently doesn't live too far away though. Brookhaven, I think."

"Ah, a yuppy area. Must have some money then."

"More than me at least."

"You got a pic?"

"No, he doesn't have a pic. She probably lives in Canada, near Niagara Falls or some shit too. Ha ha!" Bob interjects.

The weed has definitely gotten to him. He's all the way up—sky high and won't come down for a while.

Ernie gets a good laugh out of Bob's comment. I'd feel defensive if I weren't fairly stoned, so I choose to laugh as well. I know the truth, and she'll arrive around 8:00 p.m. Then I'll have the last laugh. Or at least some company and a story for tomorrow.

"No pic?" asks Ernie.

"I just met her last night. Listen …"

I lose my train of thought.

"Listen? Yeah?" asks Bob.

"Fuck it. All you need to know is she'll be here after the game, and then y'all got to go."

"Word. I hear ya. We're just fucking with ya," Ernie assures me. "Good luck tonight."

"Yeah you'll be fine. Just don't be yourself," Bob reminds me.

"Noted. I'll be Mike."

"Who's Mike?" asks Ernie.

"I don't know, but he sounds like a cool guy."

"Homey, you're higher than giraffe pussy!" Ernie proclaims laughingly.

"You're right. C'mon. Let's go inside and fuck with the jukebox."

14

Back inside the pub, Ernie, Bob, and I are hovered around the juke-box, scanning possible tunes. So many options and so few dollars, at least in my pockets. The main struggle is finding the most appropri-ate tracks to fit the mood of the bar. It's a higher energy afternoon with people excitedly watching the Braves-Mets rivalry game, so some more upbeat music will suite the patrons best.

I put a couple of dollars in the jukebox and select songs to play over the pub's PA system.

"Y'all good with some older stuff?" I ask Bob and Ernie as I make my selections.

"Yeah, works for me, man. You got this," Ernie replies.

"Make sure you play some Iggy," Bob demands.

"Already ahead of you, muchacho."

I have the songs picked for the next twenty minutes or so—"Jack & Diane" by John Cougar Mellencamp; "Superstition" by Stevie Wonder; "Heroes" by David Bowie; and finally, "Lust for Life" by Iggy Pop. The other patrons should appreciate these picks. And if not, well, screw 'em. They'll have their turn at DJ in less than half an hour. I press play, and the opening riff and hand claps of "Jack & Diane" vibrate throughout the pub. Random drinkers at the bar and tables clap in beat with the track. Minus Baby Baby, whose hand is shaking too much to properly clap in coordination.

We return to our seats at the bar and continue watching the game. Our drinks are still cool, and our stools are still warm from ass heat. We each suck down more gulps from our beverages. With the music playing and morale of the bar patrons slightly more heightened, all seems well.

"Interesting mix of songs, Matt," Bob proclaims.

"You gotta have variety, Bobert. Gotta have variety."

"I can dig it," Ernie offers.

"It's all building up to a big finish, once this mix is finished."

"That being?" asks Ernie.

"You'll have to wait and see, my friend."

We refocus our attention to the TV behind the bar. Still 0–0 in the bottom of the third with two outs. No one on base. The Braves' pitcher throws out a couple of fastballs, bringing the count to zero balls and two strikes. Another ball releases from the pitcher's hand. A curveball. This one hangs up in the zone, and the Mets' batter hammers it into deep center field. Home run—1–0 Mets.

"Motherfucker!"

"Wooo! How ya like that, Matt?" Les cheers.

"Enjoy it while it lasts, counselor."

"Oh, I will enjoy it, my boy. I'll enjoy it quite a bit."

I take a large swig of beer and notice it's slightly warmer than it had been minutes ago. It tastes like a slow defeat. Time for a change. I swallow the hot liquid defeat and order another Coors Light from Tyler. Hopefully this one will stay cooler a little longer.

As Tyler fetches my next beer, the eczema on my lower leg itches again. I'm irritated now on all fronts. This better come to an end before Holly gets here. An itchy, stoned, and drunk mess is not what she signed up for tonight, and I plan on delivering my strongest efforts. I hope.

15

The ballgame is now in the top of the fifth inning, and it's still 1–0 Mets. The Braves are taking the mound. One in the batter's box and another warming up, taking practice swings with a weight around his bat. Another handsome Brave is gearing up to receive the opening pitch—a young rookie from South America. The kid is blessed with immense potential and is developing a reputation for having a quick bat, complemented with power to boot. New York's pitching Thor winds up and throws a fastball straight down Broadway. The Braves' rookie takes the strike. Thor throws another strike low and away. The Braves' rookie hesitates, swings, and misses. He was expecting a breaking ball. The catcher lobs the ball back to the pitcher's mound and adjusts his crotch as he leans back into his stance. The young South American Brave quickly calls timeout and steps back from the batter's box, contemplating the next pitch. It's a zero-two count and Thor has pitches to burn. Looks like he might throw a breaking ball. The rookie reenters the batter's box and prepares to receive the next pitch. Thor winds up again, lunges forward, and unloads. Breaking ball. The rookie locks in and makes contact. The ball soars into deep right field and bangs off the foul pole. Home run! The Braves are now on the board. It's 1–1 and all tied up, with zero outs and at least three more handsome batters energized to take the plate. The fans in the stands on TV go berserk in celebration, as does the majority of the bar patrons in the Royal Tree. Minus Les.

"Hell yeah!"

"See ya!" yells Ernie.

"I had a feeling he had a dinger in him today," Bob proclaims in hindsight.

"Ha! Baby, I told ya boys these games are fixed. Just when one team is down, the other comes right back to keep it close. Keep ya watching," Baby Baby chimes in.

"Yeah that's how competition tends to work, Baby Baby." I reply.

We disregard Baby Baby's comment and choose to keep the positive vibes for the Braves going and cheers with our drinks, guzzling them down in celebratory fashion.

Our spirits lifted and me another step closer to a fresh twenty-dollar bill, courtesy of Les, I turn to Les and give him a thumbs-up. "Hope you're keeping that twenty dollars warm and crisp for me, Les."

"Don't get cocky, Matt. There's still a lot of game left to be played," Les answers.

"Not cocky, just confident. Looks like Thor isn't invincible after all, and I don't see any other Avengers in the bullpen."

"We'll see about that, wiseass."

"Ha ha. Cheers, guys," I say, raising my cold bottle of Coors Light to Dane and Les.

They return the gesture, and we resume watching the game.

The next few batters aren't quite as lucky as the young rookie. The next batter is overconfident and strikes out on three straight pitches. Shit. Two more outs left this inning. The next batter reaches base on balls. I'll take that.

Following him is possibly the most handsome member of the Braves. Another young player with talent. You can see the female fans blush as he takes the plate. Hopefully he can swing his bat as good as he most assuredly swings his dick. Thor stands on the mound and takes the signs from the catcher. He shakes off the first sign before settling on another pitch call. Thor lifts his leg and throws in a fastball. Straight gas. The young Brave swings, making contact, and sends a chopper down the third base line. The third baseman rushes forward, picking up the ball, and quickly throws it in to second base. Runner out. The second baseman then turns the ball and throws to first base. Runner out. The Mets turn a double play. End of the top of the fifth. Thor escapes the inning, relatively unscathed, with the exception of the homer.

"Son of a bitch!"

"Of course, he hits into a double play," Ernie announces.

"Hey, cut Mr. Handsome some slack. He's just trying his best," Bob says sarcastically.

"Oh, fuck him."

"Ha ha. Maybe if he wasn't thinking about getting laid after the game, he could've advanced the runner," Ernie states.

Baby Baby turns toward our end of the bar and continues his rabble-rousing.

"I told ya, they gonna make 'em keep it close. Ratings, baby. Ratings," Baby Baby adds.

"You know you sound like a real horse's ass when you make comments like that?" Les tells Baby Baby.

"Open your eyes, baby! It's all a multimedia ploy to keep ya distracted is all. You know about the media. Don't ya, Les?" Baby Baby fires back with a subtle remark that can only be construed as vaguely anti-Semitic, given Les's Jewish heritage.

"Piss off, Baby Baby. I don't have to listen to your shit," Les returns.

"Ha ha ha! He knows. Oh, he knows," Baby Baby says, turning away from Les and the rest of our group.

We sit in silence, briefly, trying to comprehend Baby Baby's insinuations toward Les. The more I stew on the matter, the angrier

I become with myself for not unloading on Baby Baby. As Les's friend and potentially future employee, I feel like I let him down. Putting my eventual employment status at risk. Fuckin' Baby Baby. I'll have to wait until he says something next time. If there is one. My job may depend on it. The itching on my leg returns. Must be a psychosomatic irritation manifesting from my emotions of self-hate and shame that've overtaken me following the Baby Baby v. Les spat. I take a long drink of beer and scratch.

Suddenly, there's a loud commotion at the other end of the bar. We all look to see what it's about. A large man with a distinctive voice is in the middle of unloading his frustrations with the Braves' batters on his female companion. He's an ogre. He's roughly forty years of age. Looks about six foot three. But it's hard to tell with him sitting down. He does appear to be every bit of 250 pounds, though, and his John Smoltz Braves' jersey is stretched out across his back, giving the impression it may be a size or two too small. His lady friend is quite the opposite. She's in her midthirties, slight, slim, feminine, and blonde. She can't weigh more than 110 pounds. But giving her credit, she's holding her own with her boo—trading verbal blows back and forth like a well-contested prizefighter.

"Don't talk to me like that, asshole!" she announces to him loudly.

"I'll talk to you anyway I want, you bitch!" he counters.

"You don't call me a *bitch*, motherfucker! Show me some respect!"

"I'd show you some respect if you weren't such a dismissive bitch, bitch!"

"Oh, I'm dismissive? Just because I don't care about your stupid baseball game as much as you do, you prick!"

"It's not stupid, whore! Maybe if you had another hobby or passion other than sucking dick, you'd be able to appreciate the game!"

"Trust me, asshole, I have passion. And it doesn't revolve around baseball, you, or your limp dick. So, you can fuck right off! I'm going outside for a smoke!"

"Good! Try not to get fucked by a random stranger on your way out!"

She walks away from the confrontation and heads out the front door of the pub, standing outside on the patio, lighting up a Marlboro 100, and taking long aggressive drags from the cigarette. She's clearly trying to calm her nerves. The fact that she hasn't left on her own proves a couple of things: (1) She didn't drive here, and (2) she gets off on the chaos.

Bob, Ernie, Dane, Les, and I remain seated on our stools. Stunned at what we just witnessed and shocked that no one tried to intervene. Another missed opportunity on my part. Though who would get involved? Given the size of the ogre. Also, based on his accusations of whore-ish activity on her part, she may have cheated on him at some point in the past. Love makes people crazy at times. Still, there's no reason to air dirty laundry in public.

Bob, Ernie, and I look back in Dane and Les's direction. Dane is struggling to hold back his laughter as he takes a drink of scotch and water. Les can't help but shake his head in disapproval.

"My god, what the hell was that about?" questions Les.

"I don't know. But on that note, I'm gonna have a smoke," Dane announces, rising from his stool and stepping outside for a Camel Crush.

"Why did that guy's voice sound so familiar?" asks Bob.

"He's a sports radio DJ," Les answers.

"What's his name?"

"I'm not sure what his actual name is, but he goes by Wreck Davies."

"Holy shit, are you serious? That's Wreck Davies?" Bob asks, realizing he's heard the name before.

"Who's Wreck Davies?" inquires Ernie.

"He's the sports guy on 99.7 FM. He does all the color

commentary for local Atlanta sports teams and the postmatch syn-opsis for wrestling pay-per views," Bob confirms.

"Oh, shit. That's right. I have heard of that guy. My dad listens to him in the mornings," Ernie suddenly realizes.

"Never heard of him."

"Well of course you haven't. He's not on college rock AM radio, you fucking hipster," Bob responds teasingly.

"Yeah, homey. Get with the program. He's a big deal on the radio here," Ernie adds on.

"Hmm, I'll pass."

"Don't worry. I'm with you on this one, Matt. He's a putz. All he does is bitch nonstop. No wonder his wife probably cheats on him. Ha ha." Les laughs.

"That's his wife? Fuck, she's a smoke show," Bob remarks.

"Ha, yeah. You may have a shot," Les replies.

"Maybe I'll go have a smoke break too. Ha," Bob returns with lust in his eyes.

"Have at it, homey. Ha," Ernie encourages Bob.

"Well, on that note, I'm gonna step outside for a bit," Bob announces.

"Good luck."

Bob lifts up from his stool, carrying his vodka soda with him, and exits the pub for the front patio. Les, Ernie, and I laugh and shake our heads. We watch Bob through the pub window approach the damsel in distress and motion to her for a cigarette. We each turn back to our beverages and suck down some more booze.

"I didn't know Bob smoked?" asks Ernie.

"He doesn't," I reply, taking another sip of beer. "He just loves pussy."

"So do I, but not enough to get my ass kicked over it. Wreck sees that shit, and he's gonna be pissed and ready to fuck Bob up."

"I guess that's what separates us from Bob. Lack of fear. He's the type of guy who would cross a busy highway if he knew there was snatch on the other side."

Ernie and Les laugh. We take another look out the window. Bob is smoking a Marlboro 100 and chatting up Wreck's wife. Dane remains in the opposite corner of the patio, smoking his Camels and observing a potentially problematic encounter. I'm not surprised in the least.

16

It's now 5:45 p.m. and the Royal Tree remains at half capacity. There's tension in the atmosphere. Les v. Baby Baby. Wreck Davies v. his wife. Me v. time. Another outburst has yet to occur, despite the feeling of a confrontational situation potentially exploding at any moment. Combustion could transpire, and the idea of standing or sitting near the blast is uninspiring. Nevertheless, the fuse is lit, but the sparks have yet to reach the dynamite. For now.

Wreck's wife is back inside the pub sitting next to her bombastic husband. There's little more than a few words spoke between them. Wreck's wife gives her husband a little taste of the silent treatment, and he is less than amused. Occasionally, he'll ask her who she was talking to outside, and she gives little in return for responses.

"Who was that you were talking to out there?" asks Wreck.

"Nobody."

"Looked like you were being pretty familiar."

"Mmm."

"That's all you have to say? Mmm? Who is he?"

"Some guy bumming a smoke."

"That better just be the case."

"It is."

"Good."

She remains silent, offering no reply.

"You just watch yourself. Don't embarrass me in here, or you'll be walking your ass home."

"Just watch your game."

Wreck sighs, annoyed, and orders a Bud Light from Tyler. Tyler reaches into the refrigerator below the bar and removes a longneck of Bud Light. She places the beer in front of Wreck, with a coaster underneath, and checks on the situation. "Everything good here?"

"We're fine," Wreck grunts.

"Okay. Just checking. Everyone just be cool, and we're all good."

"I got her in line."

Tyler nods her head, definitely irritated by Wreck's curtness. She leaves the conversation and exits the bar area to checks on other customers sitting at tables. She takes their requests for cheese fries and mozzarella sticks and delivers the orders to the kitchen staff.

Bob, Ernie, and I are back together at the bar—Bob having just returned from outside, after schmoozing with Wreck's wife. Ernie and I have our curiosity stricken and we have to ask Bob about what was spoken between him and Wreck's ole lady.

"So, muchacho, what happened out there?"

"Just a friendly chat between two adults," Bob replies.

"Looked like there was more than a 'friendly chat' occurring from our end," Ernie says.

"Ha. Well, it definitely felt very flirty," Bob answers.

"You put the charm on her?"

"Oh, you know it, mijo. I laid it on pretty thick," Bob confidently divulges.

"And? How'd she respond?" asks Ernie.

"Oh, very, very well, ha ha." Bob laughs.

"What'd you say to her?"

"I just asked her for a cigarette and told her I'd overheard her and Wreck arguing, and I wanted to make sure she was okay," Bob tells us.

"And?" Ernie inquires, looking for further details.

"And I told her that she was too pretty to have to take his shit, even if he's on the radio. It doesn't matter, and I will be here to make sure things don't get too heated again," Bob says with a devilish grin on his face.

"Shit, this muthafucka is putting on a white knight front for her. Ha ha." Ernie laughs.

"You got some balls on you to hit on some guy's wife practically right in front of him."

"You best believe I do, mijo." Bob smiles.

"You better watch your ass, Bob. He's a big guy. If you piss him off, he's bound to come over here and whoop the shit outta you," Ernie warns Bob.

"Ha, whatever. I could take him. Besides, it's not like I'm gonna make a move on her. Not in front of him at least. Ha," Bob responds, still with a suspicious grin across his face, making him appear like the Cheshire cat.

"I guess we'll see about that. I don't want you to cause a ruckus in here. I have a date later, and last thing I need is us getting kicked outta here because you try to go toe-to-toe with a sports DJ."

"Nothing's gonna happen. We're good. I was just planting seeds is all. Ha," Bob says, reassuring me of his intentions, which seem skeptical at best.

"You get her name?" asks Ernie.

"Angela. Angela Davies," Bob answers.

"The first lady of local Atlanta radio DJs. Hope it works out. Though, I seriously doubt it."

"You gotta have faith, bro. Like George Michael said," Bob replies.

"Didn't he die of a drug overdose?"

"It still doesn't change the message, mijo," Bob retorts.

Ernie and Bob laugh at the response. I take another swig of beer, and we look down the bar toward Wreck and Angela. They continue to sit in silence as he watches the game. She must notice our gaze because, soon after our eyes lay their presence on her, she turns her head and smiles back. Flirtatiously. I'm guessing that was for Bob. This could end poorly.

We return our gaze toward the TV screen—watching the baseball game with peaked interest. Now it's the bottom of the seventh inning, and the score is still 1–1, but the Mets have runners on second and third with one out. The next New York batter comes up to the plate and swings at the first pitch, knocking it into shallow left field and driving in a run. The game is now 2-1 Mets.

"Goddamn it."

"Ah ha! Time to blow this one wide open!" Les jeers.

"Hey, you be quiet over there. This is Braves country," Ernie remarks to Les teasingly.

"Ha ha. You can't keep New York down for long, son," Les laughingly returns.

"That post-9-11 rah-rah has run its course, homey," Ernie remarks.

"Oh my God, you really went there?" Les asks, disapprovingly.

"Sorry. That was cold-blooded. I'll take that one back. Ha," Ernie replies, his gesture revoking his former comment.

"Well shit. They're gonna pull him." I observe.

The Braves' manager jogs onto the field and signals to the bullpen that it's time to send in a relief pitcher.

"Looks like your guy is finally hitting the showers," Les remarks.

"Yeah, yeah. There's still more to play."

"I wish you luck with that shoddy relief staff you boys have. Ha ha," Les replies.

The game cuts to a beer commercial while the Braves' reliever jogs out to the mound for a few warm-up pitches. I finish off my Coors Light and wave to Tyler to bring me a new bottle. Tyler pulls out a beer from the fridge below the bar, pries off the cap with her metallic bottle opener, and places the drink on my existing coaster. I hand over my empty bottle. The mountains are pale white.

"Hey, just letting you guys know, my shift is ending soon. So, if you wouldn't mind closing out with me, I'd appreciate it," Tyler politely asks.

"Yeah, no problem."

"Yeah, we got you," Ernie confirms.

"Sure thing. Can I get a Double-Doozy burger with fries before you check out?" asks Bob.

"Cool, thanks. Yeah, I got ya. I'll get your check and be right back with your food," Tyler tells Bob.

Tyler walks back to the register, inputs Bob's order, rings up our bills, and drops the checks off for us to review. I glance down at the waxy paper. All looks good. I hand over my credit card for Tyler to complete the transaction, and Bob and Ernie follow suit. As I wait for Tyler to bring the receipts, I take a sip from the warm Coors Light. Sucking it down with contempt, I worry this is the last beer I'll have before the Mets widen the lead. Tyler returns with the receipt and pen. I sign, leaving a 20 percent tip and thanking her for the service. Bob and Ernie do the same, leaving similar tip amounts.

As Tyler walks away to gather the rest of her checks from the other patrons, I notice a silence among our group. It's clear Ernie notices the quietness too. As we look to Bob for confirmation, he has his eyes locked in on Angela Davies. He smiles at her, and she returns the favor, offering a quick wink in his direction.

"Watch yourself, muchacho."

"What?" asks Bob.

"You know what. Just be careful. Don't do anything stupid."

"I can't help it, man. It's like she's locked in on me. The bitch is in heat," Bob observes.

"Just don't start any shit in here. I got money on this game, and I don't plan on getting kicked out before I see the outcome."

"Chill out. Her guy doesn't notice a thing. He's totally glued to the TV," Bob reasons.

"Just be safe, okay?"

"I'm Mr. Safe, bro," Bob says, brushing off my request.

"Yeah, you need to wait for your burger and munch down on some grub and let this one go," Ernie tells Bob, backing me up.

"I only hope it's enough to satisfy my hunger, if you know what I mean?" Bob asks rhetorically.

"Let us pray," Ernie responds, slightly worried.

The flirty looks progress, and everyone on our end of the bar with half a sense of awareness is concerned. Bob is playing with fire and there's a better than not chance someone is going to get burned. I just have to make sure it isn't me.

17

About ten more minutes pass, and in walks Kate—the head bartender and general manager of the Royal Tree. She's the queen bee of the pub. She isn't the owner, but every regular is aware of her status. The HBIC. No one knows exactly how long Kate has worked at the Royal Tree, for she proceeds every regular in time served. Like Morgan Freeman in *Shawshank Redemption*, she's existed here for decades, no one knows what brought her to this establishment, and she's the true gatekeeper and provider of all services needed.

She's in her late forties, has blonde hair and a raspy voice, wears spectacles around her ears, and dons a no-nonsense attitude. However, she treats the regulars as if they were her own children— checking in on us, giving us rides home, offering words of advice, and especially coddling us when we're down on our luck.

In many ways, we are her adopted children—metaphorically left by our families on the Royal Tree doorstep, embraced by the warmth of Kate, and raised as her own. Kate watches out for us, and every year on one of the regular's birthday, she gives us a pint of our favorite beer on the house with a candle taped to the glass. It's a small gesture, but it means the world to those spending their days of birth in the pub, surrounded by the company of strangers and other barstool junkies.

As Kate enters the pub, she confidently struts around to the back of the bar. She rests her purse on a shelf underneath the register and punches in on her time card. It's the beginning of her shift, signifying the end of Tyler's. Kate will take it from here. After settling in, Kate waves hello to Dane, Les, Bob, Ernie, and myself. We're thrilled to see her here, for we know we're in for heavy pours of liquor and the coldest of beers—straight from the back of the fridge.

"Hey, guys," Kate says.

"Hi, Kate!" We all say, almost in unison. Like a chorus of grade school students greeting their teacher for the day.

"How's it going?" Dane asks Kate.

"It's going. Just here for the night with you gentlemen. Ha." Kate slightly chuckles.

"Well, happy to have you join us. Ha ha." Dane laughs in return.

As Tyler resets the register and counts out her tips for the day, Kate makes the rounds in the kitchen, greeting the staff and checking in on open orders. It's her due diligence that allows this operation to run so smoothly. It's like watching a mob boss greet the underlings in a movie. The mere presence of the headcheese puts everyone in check.

Once the register is reset, Tyler punches out on her time card. Kate returns from the kitchen and stacks freshly cleaned pint glasses behind the bar. A member of the kitchen staff announces loudly, "Order up!" It's Bob's Double-Doozy burger with fries.

Before Tyler leaves, she paces back to the kitchen and retrieves the entrée. She brings it straight to where we're seated and places the plate in front of Bob, along with silverware, ketchup, and mustard.

"Double-Doozy with fries. All set?" asks Tyler.

"Yup, thanks!" says Bob.

"Perfect. Well, I'm going to pack up and head out. It's been good seeing you guys!" says Tyler enthusiastically. Happy to be off work.

"Yeah good seeing you too. You gonna stick around to watch the rest of the game with your favorite customers?" I ask.

"Umm … yeah sure. Why not. I'm gonna go to the bathroom and step outside to have a smoke, and then I'll come back in for the ninth inning," Tyler says assuring us of her eventual return.

"Cool, see ya in a sec."

Tyler leaves the bar area and enters the ladies' room for her first bathroom break all day. I wouldn't believe she could hold her bladder that long if it wasn't for the fact that I've been known to hold my piss for hours on end, even after consuming a level of booze that matches the subject of Chumbawamba's song "Tubthumping."

Bob wastes no time ingesting the double burger. It's a doozy too—two patties topped with cheese, onion rings, and potato bread buns. If he finishes it, I'll be shocked. If he doesn't, I won't be surprised. Either way, his colon is in for a workout later.

We return to watching the game. Bob is systematically dismantling the double patty burger, bite by bite. It's impressive to witness. One would assume he should get a free t-shirt for consuming such a hefty sandwich.

The game is now in the later innings. Top of the eighth, to be precise. The Braves' reliever was able to get out of the inning without relinquishing any additional runs. The score remains 2-1 in the Mets favor with two outs remaining in the top half of the inning. The Braves' all-star first baseman is up to bat. He's oh to three on the day with two strikeouts and is desperate for a hit. The club needs him to show up now and earn his paycheck. I need him to show up now and earn my winnings for the day. He takes the first couple of pitches from the New York Thor, who remains in the game, despite a high pitch count. Both are curveballs that the Braves' first baseman holds off of as they break outside the strike zone.

"Good eye. Good eye," Ernie says, encouraging the Braves' batter.

"C'mon, give him something to hit," I mutter.

Thor's next pitch is a changeup that hangs high in the strike zone. The Braves' batter jumps on the pitch and fouls it off to deep left field, narrowly missing the foul pole and a game-tying home run. Even on the TV, we can see the relief in Thor's eyes as he watches the ball fly foul.

"Ah, damn it. I thought that was gone."

"That was close," Ernie replies.

"So close," Bob says with a mouth full of burger.

"Close but no cigar, boys," Les reminds us.

It's a two-to-one count, and it looks like Thor is tiring out. He's most likely one base runner away from being pulled by his manager. Thor wipes the sweat from his brow and readies himself for his 120th pitch of the game. He winds up and delivers a fastball, low and inside. The Braves' batter, brimming with confidence, swings and makes contact, driving the ball into deep left field. The ball misses becoming a home run but bounces off the outfield wall. The Brave takes off running. He rounds first base and heads for second, sliding in and picking up a one-out double off the Mets' pitcher. The crowd and the Royal Tree jeer in excitement.

"Fuck yeah!"

"Son of a bitch!" Les yells, showing signs of frustration.

"This is turning out to be one helluva game," Dane announces, commenting for the first time in a while.

Ernie, Bob, and I are equally excited to see the Braves with a runner in scoring position and the winning run coming to the plate.

The Mets' manager emerges from the dugout and jogs to the mound, tapping his arm, signaling for their first relief pitcher all game to head out to the mound. Thor's day is over. He pitched a hard-fought game, but he's out of juice. Everyone has his or her limits. The game cuts to a commercial. Ernie and I breathe a sigh of relief now that Thor is out of the game as Bob takes the last bites of his double burger and fries. Pushing the plate away, he leans back on his stool, waving the napkin as if it were a white flag.

Bob, Ernie, and I resume drinking throughout the commercial break. From the back of the pub, we hear Tyler leave the ladies' room and proceed out the back-door exit, presumably for her afore-mentioned smoke break. A minute passes by, and next Baby Baby, in a drunken stupor from too many John Daly's, stands up from his stool and stumbles out the back door exit as well. Odd, consider-ing the only people who ever leave out the back are staff members and food or liquor delivery men. Our senses are heightened by this development, and we turn to Les and Dane to see if they noticed something as well.

"Did you see that?" asks Les.

"Yeah. Why did Baby Baby go out the back door?" Dane wonders.

"That's strange. Tyler just went out there too," Les continues to observe.

"You don't think …" Dane insinuates.

"I hope not," Les says, sounding worried.

Les stands up from his stool and walks toward the back of the pub. Clinched fists and nervous demeanor carry him the whole way. He steps out the rear exit, and the rest of us wait.

Bob, Ernie, Dane, and I are left to sit and ponder what's trans-piring. Something isn't right. The four of us exchange looks of understanding. The only kind of communication that is conveyed through eye contact between men who know trouble is in the midst.

"I'm gonna go check this out to be safe," I announce.

"We'll go with you," Dane says in solidarity.

Dane, Ernie, and Bob stand from their seats and follow me through the pub toward the back door. My heart is racing. I ha-ven't felt cardiac pumps this ferocious since right before I beat Trey McNelly's ass in the tenth grade. My legs begin to itch again. The uneasiness of what I'm afraid I'm going to witness is crawling through my skin, and there's no time to scratch.

We reach the rear exit. I take a deep breath and push the door open. The door latch clicks so loudly I assume the noise can be heard all the way in Nashville. The door opens outward, and I can hear a skirmish developing between Baby Baby, Les, and Tyler. Baby Baby has Tyler's arm in his hand as Tyler is desperately trying to push away.

"I said leave me alone!" screams Tyler, throwing her cigarette in Baby Baby's face.

"Ya goddamn bitch!" cries Baby Baby.

"Get the hell outta here, Baby Baby!" yells Les, grabbing Baby Baby by the back of the shoulder.

"Shut the fuck up! No one invited your Jew ass," Baby Baby commands, swiping Les's hand off him.

"Just go back inside, Baby Baby!" Tyler desperately pleads.

"I'll go back inside after ya dance with me and give me some sugar," Baby Baby says, turning back to Tyler.

"No one's dancing with anyone. Go back inside and get the hell outta here!" Les bravely demands.

Baby Baby turns back toward Les and shoves him to the ground. Les lands on his butt. Dane, Bob, and Ernie help Les to his feet.

I step forward. "Hey, motherfucker! Leave them alone and get your hick ass outta here!"

"Oh yeah, and what the fuck are you gonna do, slim?" asks Baby Baby.

"Nothing, as long as you go."

"All I came out here to do was to have a li'l dance with Tyler over here," Baby Baby says again.

"You need to go!" Tyler yells at Baby Baby.

"I'll go when I'm good and goddamn ready to. And when did you turn out to be a mouthy cunt, after all?" Baby Baby screams.

"Watch your mouth, hillbilly!" Les yells back at Baby Baby.

"Yeah, just get the fuck out of here. You're not welcome here anymore!" Tyler yells.

"All right, fine! I'll get outta here after I kick this fuckin' kike's ass!" Baby Baby screams.

Baby Baby charges Les, arm curled back with a clinched fist raised. I push Les aside and take the hit. Baby Baby connects on the top corner of my left eyebrow. I stumble backward yet barely feel the pain, numb from the booze I've consumed throughout the evening. Baby Baby looks stunned, seeing as he hit the wrong man. Bob and Ernie step forward to defend me.

"Wait, wait!" I demand, waving my hand at Bob and Ernie to get them to hang back.

I stand back up. "That all you got, Baby Baby?"

Baby Baby, clearly pissed by my question, charges me again. He hits me with an overhand right in the same spot as before. I bend at the waist, holding my head. Baby Baby grabs me by the hair and raises his left fist to hammer punch me once again.

I swing upward with my right hand and deliver a thunderous blow to his abdomen. Baby Baby grunts and bends at the waist. I stand upright vigorously, adrenaline pumping through my veins. I grab Baby Baby by the ears, pulling them outward, and headbutt his nose. Baby Baby's head springs backward like a bobblehead, blood exploding out his nostrils and splattering across his face and mine. Some of Baby Baby's blood flies onto my lips. I taste it with my tongue. Pure animalistic energy pulsates throughout my body. My mind is clear, and every worry of love, pain, loss, and finances has dissipated. The itching on my legs disappears, and for the first time in I don't know when, I feel free.

Baby Baby gathers himself and stumbles toward me, covered in blood from nose to shirt. Desperate to end the fight, I quickly decide on my finishing maneuver. Baby Baby lifts his fist a third time, looking to land another overhand right. I block his fist with my left arm, raise my right leg, and unload a lifetime of frustration into his crotch—kicking him squarely in the dick and balls. Baby Baby instantly drops to his knees and vomits up John Dalys and defeat.

"You done?" I ask Baby Baby as he writhes in pain on all fours on the pavement.

No answer from my foe. Just the sounds of humbling anguish echoing from his mouth. I step backward to my friends.

Even in their company, I'm internally alone right now. No one can comfort or tame the rage inside me in this moment. The thrill of victory is only matched by the fear of the level of hate I am capable of. My eyes well up, and I feel as if I could cry from the overflow of emotion. I hold back the tears and stumble toward the rear entrance. My work here is done. Bob, Dane, Ernie, and Les are silent. Not a shock considering the brutality they just witnessed. They follow behind me, back into the pub.

Tyler is the only one as emotional as I am. She leans in toward Baby Baby but from a distance. "Go home, Baby Baby. It's over. And don't come back," Tyler says in a moment of catharsis, before turning away and following the rest of us back into the pub.

We reenter the Royal Tree, leaving Baby Baby to bleed in the alleyway out back.

"I'm gonna need a minute, guys," I let everyone know.

Bob, Ernie, Dane, and Les nod their heads and return to their bar stools. Tyler hangs back and hugs me. No words are exchanged. We relinquish our embrace. She slowly walks back to the bar. I enter the men's room to have some time alone to myself.

As I stand at the sink in the men's room, washing the blood from my face, I can't help but feel worried about what transpired and the consequences. Charges? Jail time? Civil suit? What happens next?

I splash water and soap on my face, cleansing myself of the past—a baptism of such. I beg for forgiveness from a God in which I'm not sure I believe. I wipe my face with paper towels stacked on the sink and look at my face in the mirror. My left eye is bruised and swelling. Panic swarms my senses. I'm supposed to meet Holly soon. What will she think of this? I can't let her know what happened. This whole incident needs to be wiped from the record as far as she's concerned. Only thing to do now is get something cold on the eye. I wish I had a rare steak or a bag of peas to apply to the swelling and relieve the symptom. A cool Coors Light should suffice though. I exit the men's room, head down, and return to my stool. Bob, Dane, Ernie, and Les remain silent. Tyler is nowhere to be seen. She's officially left. Understandable.

I sit on the stool and wave to Kate. She already has her eyes on me. Kate reaches in the fridge, pulling out a Coors Light, and drops it off in front of me at the bar.

"Good job, Matty," Kate says and walks away.

Clearly, she has already gotten word of the brawl—from Tyler presumably. I'm surprised I haven't been asked to leave, but something tells me Kate had plans of taking out the trash eventually anyways. I just saved her the trip. I pick up the beer and take a drink.

Les leans in to reassure me everything is okay—father figure like. "Don't worry, son. There were plenty of people out there who saw what happened. Self-defense. If you need anything, let me know. I'll back you up," Les says.

"Thanks, Les. I appreciate it."

Bob and Ernie look me in the eyes and wink approvingly. I feel respected for the first time in lord knows how long. I pick the bottle of Coors Light back up and take another swig. The beer tastes better than anything I've drunk all day. It feels earned. Like it was worth it. Like I'm worth it. I look at the mountains on the bottle. They're bluer than Frank Sinatra's eyes. I press the chilled bottle to my left eye and look back to the TV, checking the score of the game.

18

Sitting at the bar, still with the chilled beer to my eye, I watch the last inning of the Braves v. Mets game. I'm flanked once again by Dane and Les to my left and Bob and Ernie to my right. While we were outside, the Braves tied the game up, 2–2, in the eighth inning after a sac fly that sent the Braves' runner from second to third base, followed by a wild pitch, which led to the lone base runner stealing home. A calamity of errors by the New York squad has put the Braves back in the game, and now the top of the ninth inning is underway. It's a shame we missed the tying run come across home plate. But a lady was in need, and briefly, I was able to play the part of Batman. Not a bad trade.

The first two Braves' batters go down swinging at the hands of the Mets' veteran closer and one out remains in the top of the ninth. Next up is the Braves' catcher to bat. He's struggled throughout the season thus far, only batting .225 and riding a cold streak the past couple of weeks. No one is expecting much out of him now. I've been there before. If it wasn't for decimating Baby Baby in the back alleyway only minutes ago, I would still relate to the catcher's plight. But sometimes all it takes is one good swing to put yourself back on top. Or in my case, a kick from the depths of hell.

The Mets' closer throws pitch number one to the Braves' catcher, and he takes a ball one on a low-breaking sinker in the bottom left corner of the strike zone. Count is now 1–0. The closer throws in his next pitch. It's a fastball intended for the lower left corner of the plate, but this time the Braves' catcher jumps on it and sends a blooper over the Mets' infield and drops in front of the right fielder. Base hit. The Braves' catcher is now on first base and represents the winning run.

The Royal Tree patrons jeer once more, clapping but still holding back on a full explosion of joy. The win is in reach, but there's still another batter yet to hit. Even still, there's an appreciation in the air for the clutch hit by the Braves' catcher. Looks like both of us have had a breakthrough tonight.

Ernie, Bob, and I take more sips of our beers as the Braves' manager signals to the umpire for a pinch hitter in place of the next batter. Walking into the batter's box now is a Braves rookie, recently called up to the majors after a stellar showing in the AAA league. He's off to an equally promising start to his major league career this season, batting .275 with three home runs and eight RBIs in just fifteen games with the club. The kid isn't a looker like the majority of his teammates, but he has power, and the Braves' manager is counting on some thunder to rumble with this at bat.

The Mets' closer stares down the young Brave. Judging from the look in his eyes, he's hell-bent on intimidating the young hitter. The Met unleashes a ninety-five-mile-per-hour fastball high and inside to the Braves' rookie. The kid is just young and cocky enough not to flinch and swings a quick bat at the first pitch. Connects. The bat makes contact with the pitch and a loud *thwack* echoes throughout the stadium. The Mets' closer mouths "Fuck!" and turns to watch the ball sail into deep right field. Going, going, gone. Home run. The fans in the stands go berserk, and tomahawk chops are seen waving throughout the stadium as two Braves round the bases for home plate. Now, with a 4–2 lead, the Braves have taken control of the game and come from behind, setting the stage for a dramatic win. The Royal Tree has erupted as well. Loud jeers and thunderous applause can be heard from the parking lot of the suburban strip mall outside.

Bob, Ernie, and I clink our drinks together and take prolonged gulps in celebration. Dane and Les, however, aren't as thrilled as us. Dane sees the Braves potentially extending their lead in the NL East by another game and Les suddenly feels twenty dollars slowly slip from his grasp.

I turn to Dane and Les to acknowledge the recent developments. "Damn, that must suck to see that ball fly outta there. I didn't think it was gonna stop until it hit I-285."

"Enjoy it while it lasts, wiseass," Les says in frustration.

"I am enjoying it, Les. I'm enjoying this quite thoroughly."

"I can't believe they blew that fucking lead," Dane says.

"It's destiny, Dane. You can't stop destiny."

"Destiny, schmestiny. Atlanta's destiny is going to be getting their asses handed to them in the playoffs," Les retorts disparagingly.

"Even if that happens, you know who won't be in the playoffs? New York and Washington. Oh, how sweet that sounds."

"Eh, screw it." Les waves me off.

I check my phone for the time—6:45 p.m. Holly should be here in the next sixty to seventy-five minutes. It's about time to start sobering up. I ask Kate for a water with no ice, and she obliges, pouring the glass of hydration from the fountain and placing it in front of me at the bar.

"You going on the wagon or something?" asks Kate.

"Ha. Never. I got a date later, and I need to be sharp."

"Ha. I see. Well, finish that water, and I'll get you a coffee to go with it," Kate says.

"Thanks, Kate."

I chug the water and feel the cool liquid wash its way down my throat and into my belly. The hydrating molecules course through my veins, and I am refreshed. As Kate fetches my coffee, I return to watching the game. The Mets' closer stays in and finishes off the inning after the next Braves' batter pops out to shallow center field. Now on to the bottom of the ninth, and the heart of the Mets' order is due up to hit. Luckily, Atlanta has a veteran closer on the mound, acquired in a trade after the all-star break, with a wicked slider and an equally devastating fastball to pair. I like our chances.

The inning proceeds as hoped. The first Mets' batter, a little too eager to get on base, goes down on three straight strikes. The next New York batter is luckier. He reaches base on balls after working the count full and taking a slider off the plate. Now, one out with a runner on first, the Mets' best hitter comes to the plate. He's nursing a .313 average and has been consistent all season, rarely falling into slumps and surgical in his ability to hit the ball into the open field. He doesn't disappoint this time either. After fouling off the first couple of pitches he sees, the Met reaches base after driving a ground single through the middle of the infield. Les is ecstatic at the play.

"Aha! That's what we pay him for!" Les announces in jubilation.

"Relax, Les. It's one hit."

"One hit that is setting up the tying run coming to the plate." Les reminds me of the stakes of the upcoming batters.

Kate returns with a steaming cup of black coffee, freshly brewed from the pot behind the bar. I sip from the cup immediately upon delivery. I burn the inside of my mouth and instantly feel the sensation of blisters forming on the membranes of my cheeks.

"Son of a bitch!"

"You dumb motherfucker," Bob says.

"Goddamn it that's fucking hot!"

"Matt," Ernie chimes in, very matter-of-fact, "it's coffee."

As the sores in my mouth and on my tongue form, I can't help but think of the old street joke: "How'd the hipster's food burn his mouth? He ate it before it was cool." Fitting.

I persevere and take another sip after blowing on the piping hot liquid in attempt to cool it off before consumption. I need to be relatively sober before Holly arrives. I can function at damn near full bore while riding a strong buzz, but true drunk leaves me with a bit too much of the case of the "fuck its." And in regard to tonight's date, I'd like to give a fuck. At least long enough to finish with pleasantries and for her to feel good and lubricated after a couple of cocktails as well. I continue to sip the coffee.

The game is now down to the final two outs of the last inning. The Braves are going to seal the win or blow the lead, resulting in a loss or extra innings. In the event of the latter, I don't have the time or the energy for either. I must save up what's left in the tank to charm a lovely lady an hour from now. A Braves triumph would certainly put a smile on my face for the meeting.

And so, the Braves closer winds up to pitch to the New York batter. Ball one on the outside corner of the plate. The next pitch, ball two on the outside corner again. It's a two-zero count, and the Braves' fan base is nervous. Walking the batter would lead to the Mets' winning run coming to the plate. The Braves' closer, in desperation for a strike, throws a fastball high in the strike zone, and it's quickly fouled off down the first baseline. Two-one count, and the Mets' batter is locked in and has proven his bat is swift enough to match the closer's fastball. The Braves' closer prepares for the fourth pitch of the at bat. He winds up again and delivers a slider to the batter, which starts in the strike zone and breaks away from the plate. The batter chases the pitch and connects, sending a chopper down the third baseline. The Braves' third baseman rushes forward, scooping up the ball and flips his wrist, sending the ball to second base. Out number two. The Mets' runner is still sprinting for first base to leg out a fielder's choice. Before he can reach the base bag, the second baseman has fired a perfect throw to first base, beating the runner to the bag. Out number three. Double play. Game over. Braves win 4–2. The Atlanta fans and Royal Tree patrons rejoice exuberantly.

"Hell yeah!"

"That a way, Bravos!" cry Bob and Ernie almost simultaneously.

"That's how it's fucking done!" yells Wreck from the end of the bar.

I turn to face Dane and Les, defeated looks upon their faces. But none such as Les. His childhood team has been left wanting, and he's on the wrong end of a wager with yours truly. There're fewer heartbreaks worse than when your team loses. Especially, when they're all you have to love.

"Hey, it was a good game at least," Dane says, trying to lessen the sting for Les.

"Yeah, yeah. Great game, my ass. Fucking Mets," Les responds sullenly.

"Hey, Les. Good game."

"Yeah, good game. I still can't believe they blew the lead like that. And to a guy in a slump and some rookie pinch hitter," Les says, shaking my hand.

"The sun even shines on a dog's ass every now and then," Dane says in condolence to Les.

Les completes our handshake. As he pulls his hand away, I open my palm, facing up, and stare. Something is missing. My payment, in full. "Hey, Les. You forgetting something?" I say, holding my hand out.

"My god. At least wait for my body to get cold before you check my pockets. Ha ha." Les laughs.

"Just don't want you running off with my due reward."

"Yeah, I'm gonna skip out on a twenty-dollar bet," Les says, opening his wallet and handing me a folded twenty-dollar bill.

"Thank you very much. Pleasure doing business with you, sir."

"Yeah, I'm sure. I wish I could say the pleasure was mutual. Ha," Les replies.

I turn back toward the bar and signal for Kate. She walks toward me, carrying another water with her. She places the water in front of me.

"Another water, I'm guessing?" asks Kate.

"Yes, a water is great. And also, could I get three shots of Jameson, too, for me and the boys here?" I ask, motioning to Bob and Ernie.

"Ha. Sure." Kate laughs.

"Also, you guys hungry?" I ask Bob and Ernie.

"Nah, man, I'm stuffed from that burger," Bob answers.

"I could eat," Ernie replies.

"Cool. Kate, how about some nachos as well for me and my friend."

"Sure. How you want them? Regular or fiesta?" asks Kate.

"I'm feeling a fiesta, Kate."

"Alrighty. Coming right up," Kate says as she walks away.

Kate returns shortly with three shots of Jameson and places them on the bar top in front of Bob, Ernie, and me. We lift our shots in the air to eye level and propose a toast.

"To the Braves, may they chop on," Ernie says.

"And to the Mets," Bob adds.

"Oh, fuck the Mets." Bob, Ernie, and I finish the toast in unison.

We throw back the shots of whiskey and wince as the liquor burns our throats on the way down. It tastes like success.

"Well, on that note, I'm gonna bid you gentlemen adieu," Les announces, standing from his stool and placing forty dollars on the bar for his tab.

Kate walks over and gathers the cash.

"Want change?" asks Kate.

"No, the rest is for you, Kate," Les says.

"Thank ya, Les. Have a good night." Kate bids Les farewell for the evening.

Les shakes hands with Dane, Bob, Ernie, and me, wishing us a good rest of the night.

Before leaving, he leans in close to my ear and reminds me to reach out to him about future work. "Matty, remember, you look for some work. But if nothing comes up, let me know and I'll see if I can pull some strings for ya. Okay?"

"Will do. Thanks, Les. I appreciate it."

"It's the least I can do. And as your attorney, I'll advise you to not get in anymore barroom scraps. But as your friend, thanks for your help out there earlier."

"Ha. Anytime, Les. You're a good guy."

"You're a real mensch as well." Les smiles at me.

Les turns and walks out the door of the Royal Tree, exiting for the night. I'm sure I'll see him tomorrow as well. Except this time, I'll be twenty dollars richer.

I pick the glass of water up from the bar and chug it. My bladder is now beyond capacity, and I'm in need of a release. I excuse myself from the bar and walk back to the bathroom. I reach the toilet and piss into the commode. My urine is loudly hitting the water of the toilet, and a sweet euphoria of a physical release floods my system as I drain the fluid from my bladder. I finish emptying the day's booze and water into the toilet and flush it away, watching my afternoon consumption spin down the drain. I zip my jeans up, making a point not to get my cock and balls caught in the fly, and wash my hands.

As I rinse the soap from my hands, I look into the mirror. My eye is swollen, and faded bruising has settled in around my eye socket. I'm going to need an excuse for this for Holly later. I check my watch—7:00 pm. One hour to come up with a reason for the contusion. Still plenty of time. I dry my hands and return to my seat at the bar, next to Bob and Ernie.

19

Ernie and I have finished off the fiesta nachos, and our bellies are full of satisfaction. The game went our way, and after a feast meant for Mexican kings, we're more than elated with the turnout this summer Saturday. Bob's stomach grumbles, and he puts his hand on his abdomen and unleashes a heavy burp. The stench of stomach gas fills the air, and Ernie and I are appalled.

"Goddamn, homey. Hold that shit in or take it outside," Ernie complains.

"My bad, bro. That burger isn't sitting well," Bob says.

"Well get some Tums or go in the bathroom and blow that shit out. No one needs to endure that mess," Ernie says.

"I second that motion."

"I'll wait until I get home," Bob tells us.

Ernie takes a sip from his beer and checks his watch.

"When you need us to leave, Matt?" asks Ernie.

"Holly ain't supposed to get here till 8:00 p.m. So, as long as y'all are out before then, we're good."

"Cool. What you say we head out around 7:45 p.m.?" Ernie suggests.

"Yeah that'd work. Sorry about kicking y'all out, but duty calls, you know what I mean?"

"Word. We got you," Ernie reassures me.

"Wanna step out for a smoke or two?"

"Yeah, I'd be down for that. Bob, you coming?" Ernie asks.

"I don't know, guys. I think I'll just sit here and chill for a sec and check Bumble," Bob says.

"Ha. Okay cool. Be back in a minute," Ernie tells Bob.

Ernie and I get up from our seats and walk outside to bum cigarettes from whoever is smoking outside. We exit the bar entrance for the front patio to find Wreck Davies and his wife, Angela, outside arguing while Wreck smokes a cigar.

"I'm ready to go," Angela says.

"I ain't leaving until I finish this cigar," Wreck tells her.

"You can smoke it at home. Let's just go. We've been here all day, and I'm ready to leave," Angela demands.

"Fuck off," Wreck says, blowing smoke in Angela's face.

It's clear the bad blood is still boiling from earlier, and Wreck is willing to throw fuel on the flames. Ernie and I look on stunned at the dick-ish behavior on the part of Wreck.

Angela storms off and reenters the pub as Dane exits to the patio for a cigarette. Angela rushes through the bar, back to her seat. "Can I get a shot of whiskey?" asks Angela.

"Jameson okay?" asks Kate.

"Fine," Angela answers.

Kate pours out a shot of Jameson and passes it to Angela.

Angela shoots the shot of whiskey back down her throat and winces from the burn of the dark liquor. She motions to Kate once more. "Let me get another?" asks Angela.

Kate picks up the bottle of Jameson and pours out another shot. She places the shot in front of Angela. And as quickly as it was poured, it goes down just as fast.

Kate is now concerned. "You okay, honey?" she asks.

"No. That asshole thinks he can treat me like shit. I'm over it. I don't give a fuck if he's on the radio or not. I don't have to put up with that crap," Angela vents.

"It's okay, darling. Here. This next one is on me," Kate says, pouring Angela another shot of Jameson.

Angela slowly picks the shooter up and drinks half the shot. She sits the shot glass down on the bar and scans the pub, now only a quarter full after the crowd in to watch the Braves game has filtered out. Her eyes land on Bob, and she stares until her glare is noticed by him.

Bob looks back in her direction and their eyes meet. He smiles. Angela smiles back. Bob winks, and Angela finishes off the shot. Kate looks on and shakes her head. She smells trouble but plays laissez-faire when it comes to interpersonal relations among the Royal Tree patrons. She won't pass judgment lest she be judged.

Outside on the patio, Ernie and I are in the process of bumming cigarettes from Dane.

"Hey, Dane, you got a couple cigs we can bum off you? We can give you a couple bucks."

"Don't worry about the money, Matt. Here ya go," Dane says, pulling two cigarettes from his pack of Camel Crush and handing them to Ernie and me.

"Thanks, man. I appreciate it."

Ernie and I put the cigarettes between our lips. I take the lighter out of my pant pocket and light up. Ernie leans in close to me, waiting for me to light his cigarette as well. I pull the lighter back and put my hand up.

"Whoa, man. You can light your own cigarette."

I hand the lighter to Ernie, and he looks confused as he lights his cigarette with my lighter. "You have something against lighting my cigarette?" asks Ernie.

"Just a rule I have, my man."

"And that is?" asks Ernie.

"There're a couple simple rules that I live by. I learned this from my cousin, Bo. One, I don't ride motorcycles nuts to butts. And two, I don't light other men's cigarettes."

Ernie and Dane laugh loudly.

"Ha ha. Okay, I can dig that," Ernie says.

"Ha. I like it. Kinda homophobic, but I like it." Dane laughs.

"Nothing homophobic about it, Dane. It's just something that a man needs to learn to do himself. Take control of your destiny. All that shit."

"I get it. You don't wanna be complicit in helping someone destroy themselves. Smoking and riding motorcycles being the potentially destructive behavior," Ernie says.

"Well said, sir. I'm no enabler. Just a provider of tools."

"Whatever helps you sleep at night. Ha ha." Dane laughs.

"Who says I sleep at night?"

Dane, Ernie, and I take drags off our cigarettes and blow the smoke into the sky, now dimming as the sun sets. It's going to be a beautiful night. I look over to Wreck as he continues to smoke his cigar—now only halfway through the bat.

Back inside the pub, Bob sips a vodka soda as he continues exchanging stares with Angela. Bob motions to Kate and requests she send another shot to Angela, on his tab. Kate pours the shot of Jameson and transfers it to Angela. Bob looks toward Angela and raises his glass to her. Angela lifts the shot and returns the gesture. Bob and Angela both down the remainder of their drinks. Bob shakes off the aftereffects of the chugged vodka as Angela does the same with her whiskey shot. After the rush of the alcohol intake has subsided, Angela removes a ballpoint pen from her purse and writes on her coaster. She picks the coaster up and stumbles down the bar in Bob's direction. As she reaches his stool, Bob swivels in his seat to face her.

"Hey," says Bob.

"Hey there. Thanks for the drink."

"No problem. It's on me."

"Ha. I figured. Here," Angela says, passing the coaster to Bob.

Bob takes the coaster from Angela and looks down at the circular cardboard. He turns it over, looking for some sort of message. He finds it on the flip side. The blue ink reads, "Meet me in the bathroom."

Bob's eyes widen, and he looks back up at Angela. She smiles seductively and turns away, walking toward the men's room. She enters the bathroom and Bob stands from his seat, equally anxious and perplexed. He turns to look back out the front window. Dane, Ernie, and I can be seen still talking as we smoke our cigarettes. Wreck continues to puff away at his Cohiba—unassuming and content, completely oblivious to Angela's actions.

Bob's stomach growls once more, and an uneasiness settles deep in his gut. *Probably just gas. Fuck it, I ain't gonna pass up a chance to get my dick wet*, he thinks.

Bob walks to the back of the pub in the direction of the men's room and catches Kate's eyes as he progresses. Her eyebrows raise slightly over her eyeglasses in acknowledgement of what is transpiring between Bob and Angela. She then turns her head away and looks up at the post–baseball game broadcast airing on TV. Hear no evil, see no evil. Plausible deniability. Bob presses forward, reaching the men's room door and enters.

Immediately after closing the bathroom door and locking it, Angela pounces on Bob. They furiously kiss, deeply their tongues deeply in each other's mouths. Their tongues massage one another's and dance between their cheeks. The make-out session is so intense they can each feel their front teeth clacking together. It's a violent, passionate embrace. Animalistic. Primal.

As they devour each other, Bob slides his right hand down the front of Angela's pants and massages her clit. She's wet and responds, opening her mouth even wider as Bob pushes his tongue deeper into her oral cavity. He pushes her up against the wall, hand still massaging her vagina, and feels her widen her legs even more so, offering Bob's fingers more space to maneuver.

Bob's cock thickens and is strong. Alert and at attention. Pressing forcefully against the zipper on the front of cargo shorts. His heightened arousal excites him. He notices droplets of premature ejaculate dribble from his urethra. Bob removes his tongue from Angela's mouth and kisses her neck and collarbone, while squeezing her right breast with his left hand.

She moans in ecstasy. "Oh, fuck. Fuck, yeah."

"You like that?" Bob whispers.

"Mmm-hmm," Angela responds, biting her lip.

Angela's breathing becomes heavier and more frequent. Bob inputs his fore and middle fingers inside Angela's opening and caresses her clit with his thumb. Her deep breathing turns to resemble panting.

"Oh, fuck. I'm gonna come. I'm gonna come," Angela announces with pleasure.

"Come for me," Bob demands.

Angela audibly moans once more, even louder than previously. Bob feels her vaginal muscles contracting on his fingers. As she climaxes, Bob slides his tongue back into Angela's mouth, now agape, and kisses her once more. Angela relaxes, and her cunt finally relinquishes its grip on Bob's fingers. She pushes him back, now at arm's length. She can't believe that a stranger in cargo shorts could ever give her an orgasm.

"That was great," she says, still breathing heavily but now more controlled.

Bob receives the affirmation. "Glad you liked that."

Angela looks down at Bob's waist area. She notices his hard dick desperately trying to poke through the fabric of his shorts. She steps toward Bob and places her hand on his cock over his shorts and begins rubbing ever so slightly. They kiss again, and she whispers in Bob's ear.

"Want me to suck your cock?" asks Angela.

"Oh yeah," Bob responds confidently.

"Take off your shorts and sit down," Angela demands.

Bob unzips his shorts and drops them down around his ankles. He steps back and sits his bare ass down on the toilet seat. Angela drops to her knees and takes his dick in her hand and proceeds to lick it from shaft to tip. Bob leans his head back in ecstasy and stares into the light fixed in the ceiling as if it were God peering down from the heavens. Angela takes his dick in her mouth and slowly bobs her head up and down, only breaking to occasionally stroke his member with her hand. *She's a pro*, he thinks as the euphoria crashes like ocean waves over his body.

Abruptly, Bob's stomach begins to turn, and the uneasy sensation returns. A pressure sets in his colon, and he detects he will need to use the bathroom very soon. He holds it in and starts to lose focus on the pleasurable fellating at hand. Angela continues to bob and stroke. She's gaining speed, and the suction of her mouth on Bob's cock is powerful enough to suck a basketball through a plastic straw. Bob struggles to hold his bowels, but the blow job is so fantastic he can't focus on anything else much longer. He puts his hands on her head and holds her hair as she sucks away.

"Oh, God. Just like that," Bob encourages.

Angela maintains her motion and presses on as instructed. Bob notices he's on the verge of climax. The blow job is hitting the peak. Bob feels the semen creeping up his shaft toward the tip of his urethra. He comes vigorously into Angela's mouth, but she doesn't stop sucking. His toes curl in his shoes as his jaw drops, and he can't take any more. His muscles relax and an overwhelming flood of shit explodes from his ass into the toilet. A full-on stream of diarrhea-like waste plows out of his body as his eyes roll in the back of his head in sweet relief.

Angela promptly concludes fellating Bob's penis and yells in horror, "What the fuck!"

"I'm sorry. I'm so sorry!" Bob says.

"You nasty motherfucker!"

"I couldn't hold it any longer! I'm sorry!" Bob begs for forgiveness.

Angela dry heaves, puts her hand over her mouth, and gags. Suddenly, a stream of vomit projectiles out her mouth and onto Bob's legs and shorts. The shock of performing a blow job with a feces-filled crescendo and the stench of shit in the air is too much for her to bear.

"Oh no!" Bob yells in disgust.

"You piece of shit!"

"Oh, Christ. I didn't mean to. I'm so sorry!" Bob says.

Angela gathers herself and makes it to her feet. She unlocks the bathroom door and storms out, leaving Bob covered in her puke and his own shit. Bob leaps off the toilet seat and shuts the door behind her, locking it once more. Desperately, he wipes his ass and scrubs the front of his shorts with hand soap in an attempt to clean himself up. Never has something so purely exulting ended so revoltingly. Definitely a result of the Double Doozy.

20

Outside on the Royal Tree patio, Dane, Ernie, and I are enjoying our prolonged smoke break. Dane, without us asking, offers up two more Camel Crush cigarettes to Ernie and me. I guess he wants us to keep him company outside. I light the cigarette with my Bic lighter and pass it to Ernie so he can do the same. I take an initial drag off the Camel and proceed to press my thumb and forefinger together on the butt of the cigarette, collapsing the menthol capsule embedded in the filter. Ernie does the same and we smoke our now menthol-transformed Camels, thoroughly enjoying the soothing minty-flavored inhale. It tastes like Christmas in August and is a more appealing scent than Wreck's Cohiba, which he carries on with, puffing away, totally unaware of what his wife has been up to in the men's room.

Abruptly, the front door of the Royal Tree flies open. Angela follows, mascara running from tears. She approaches Wreck, who's leaning against the metal fence encasing the patio and shoves him in the chest.

"You son of a bitch!" Angela screams, as if Wreck is to blame for her despair.

"What the fuck is wrong with you?" Wreck responds, equally angered and confused.

"Let's go!"

"I'm not leaving till I finish my cigar!"

"I wanted to leave before you lit that stupid thing!"

"Where's this bullshit coming from? You're acting like an insane person!"

"You calling me crazy? I'll show you crazy, motherfucker!" Angela reaches back and slaps Wreck across the face.

The force of her open hand connecting with Wreck's cheek sends the Cohiba flying from his mouth and onto the ground below. Angela cocks her hand back again, preparing for a second slap to her husband's face, and Wreck catches it midair and grabs her other arm with his opposite hand, neutralizing the attack.

Dane, Ernie, and I hang back, stunned and less than willing to interject in the domestic dispute. *One fight is enough for me this evening*, I think. Also, I know my limits. And from the size of Wreck, I would be outgunned and outmatched. David and Goliath is only a myth.

"Have you lost your fucking mind!" screams Wreck.

Angela flails about helplessly and stomps the ground in frustration. Her tears turn to sobs, and an inconsolable, embarrassing sadness overtakes her rage. Her head collapses into Wreck's chest as she drunkenly cries onto the Braves' logo smattered across the chest of his jersey.

"What's happening? Are you hammered?" asks Wreck, now more concerned than irate.

"I just wanna go home!" Angela cries, snot sniffling in her nostrils as she breathes.

"All right, all right. Fine. We'll go. Goddamn. Just let me pay the tab, and we'll go."

"Fuck the tab!" Angela screams.

"All right, fine! Fuck it. I'll come back and pay it tomorrow," Wreck says, putting his arm around Angela.

Wreck guides Angela off the patio and into the parking lot. He opens her door for her, and she sits in the passenger seat. Wreck slams the door and is heard saying "Fucking nutjob!" as he walks around the back of the car. He climbs in the driver's side, starts the engine, and drives away.

Dane, Ernie, and I look at each other, dazed and unaware of the catalyst for the event that just unfolded. We laugh and take longer drags off our Camels.

Dane ashes his cigarette with a flick of his thumb to the butt and breaks the silence. "What the fuck was that about? Ha ha." He laughs.

"Homey, I got no idea. Ha." Ernie laughs as well.

"I'm gonna need more than a few explanations."

"Speaking of, where's Bob?" asks Ernie.

"Fuck if I know. You see him inside?"

Dane, Ernie, and I look into the pub through the glass front door. There's no sign of Bob. Only Kate and a smattering of customers seated inside the pub. After a few seconds of scoping the interior, Bob emerges from the bathroom. A stupefied look is upon his face, and the front of his shorts are soaked. He barges through the bar area and proceeds outside for the patio. The front door swings open, and his facial expression has changed from stunned to a nervous smile.

"What the fuck, Bobert? Did you piss yourself?"

"Ha, no, man. Shit just got weird," Bob replies.

"Like, how weird?"

"Did you have something to do with that shit that just happened out here?" Ernie asks.

"What do you mean?" Bob asks curiously.

"Wreck's wife just ran out here and attacked him, demanding to leave. Ha ha," Dane says, explaining the previous events

"Oh, shit. I can't say I'm shocked though," Bob says.

"Ha. You have something to do with that?" asks Ernie.

"Ha. Kinda," Bob admits.

"Ah, fuckin' hell. Of course. What'd you do?"

"Well, we were hooking up—" Bob begins.

"You and Wreck's wife?" Dane asks.

"Ha. Yeah, man," Bob confesses.

"Ha ha. Goddamn, homey. You're fucked up," Ernie says.

"So, what happened?" I inquire.

"We were hooking up and she started blowing me on the toilet. And I don't know what happened, but my stomach started acting funky. And I guess when I started to come … I must've just relaxed too much and shit in the toilet mid-BJ," Bob reveals, a nervous smile smeared across his face.

"Oh!" Dane yells in disgust.

"What the fuck is wrong with you?" I ask with disdain.

"I didn't mean to!" Bob says.

"Motherfucker, you're telling us you just got a blumpkin in the bathroom?" Ernie yells.

"Shhh! Shut the hell up, man. Wreck might hear you," Bob says.

"Ha ha! Don't worry about that, Bob. They're long gone, now. Ha ha!" Dane says.

"Oh, thank God. That guy was huge, and I was getting worried he would find out," Bob says, admitting the source of his initial nervousness.

"Nah, you're all clear now, homey. But holy shit. I can't believe that just happened. Ha ha." Ernie laughs.

"Me neither. She even threw up on my shorts too," Bob continues to divulge.

"You may be the vilest human being I've ever met. And I've known some low-class assholes. Ha."

"Ha. Fuck you. Ha ha. But for real, guys. I need to go. My fucking clothes are soaked, and I need to get in the shower, ASAP," Bob tells us.

"Yeah, get outta here and wash that ass while you're at it. And throw the wash cloth away when you're done. Ha ha." Ernie tells Bob.

"Ernie, don't be ridiculous. You know white people don't use wash cloths." Bob laughs while correcting Ernie.

"Ha! True, true. Well, all right. Go on ahead and go pay your tab and bounce. I'm not far behind you either," Ernie advises Bob.

"Kay, cool. I'm gonna head back in there and pay real quick, and then I'm heading home," Bob announces.

"Cool. Do what you gotta do."

Bob reenters the pub and walks to the bar to pay his tab. Dane, Ernie, and I stay outside and laugh even more at the mess Bob has made of himself and his night. I couldn't have asked for a better story to hear. It's not every day you learn of such a deviant act. I'm just glad it didn't happen to me.

The sun is begging to set and the sky is picturesque, transitioning from vanilla to a dark blue. It's been a great day thus far. I check my watch—7:30 p.m. Holly should be arriving momentarily. I take additional pulls from my cigarette and blow the smoke into the sky, watching the blue cloud fade into the night.

Bob reemerges from the pub, and is pocketing a receipt.

"You out?" I ask.

"Yeah, man. It's a wrap on me," Bob declares.

"All right then. See ya later."

"Yeah, go home and clean up," Ernie tells Bob.

"Ha. Will do. All right. Later guys," Bob says, walking away after fist-bumping Dane, Ernie, and me.

And away he goes. Bob exits the patio and walks through the parking lot toward his SUV. The vehicle ignition turns over, and the car starts. Bob pulls out of his parking space and drives off to his suburban home. No matter how clean he may keep his residence, there's not enough bleach to sanitize the human within. Not after tonight.

Bob's put a smile on my face—one that will take a lifetime to wipe away. So, I take the final drags from my cigarette and flick the butt into the parking lot. Soaring and spinning. The amber distinguishing beautifully midair before crashing down and slowly burning out on the parking lot pavement. I'll check on Bob later after I leave the pub. Better come up with some amusing insults to fling his way. For the well of ridicule is now deep and plentiful.

21

Ernie and I are at our stool section, leaning against the bar. Dane hangs back and polishes off another Camel Crush on the patio. He's down to his final cigarette of the pack, but he's come prepared with a reinforcement pack nestled inside his fleece. He always has a backup plan. Often, I wonder if he travels with a carton, just in case. He's a man who knows how to efficiently support a habit. So, he proceeds to slowly enjoy, inhaling the final Camel among the flock.

Ernie raises his arm and gestures a signing motion, his hand holding an imaginary pen. Kate takes notice of this gesture and sets in motion the process of printing out Ernie's tab since her shift commenced. Kate approaches Ernie and me and places a bill of purchases in front of Ernie. Ernie lays down an American Express SkyMiles credit card on top of the bill before Kate can leave the scene. I take the sign of his AMEX SkyMiles card as a sign of prosperity and good fortune, meaning I won't be surprised if he feels pressured to leave a large tip.

Kate immediately takes the AMEX and tab back to the computer behind the bar and checks Ernie out for the night. Ernie signs the returned bill, leaving a hefty but fair gratuity amount, and thanks Kate for the drinks.

"You're welcome, honey," Kate says, lifting her copy of the receipt and returning back to performing her barmaid duties.

"Man, that was a helluva day, right? Ha." Ernie laughs.

"Yeah, it was. Thanks for coming out."

"And there's still much more to go for ya too."

"Yeah, man. She should be here soon."

"You nervous?"

"More excited than anything. Just hoping we have the same rapport as we had last night."

"You will. Just be yourself, homey. You'll be fine."

"Ha, yeah, well, that would be interesting. 'Myself' is an unemployed bar rat, so I hope she's into that. Ha."

"Don't talk about yourself like that, man. You got more than that going for you. You're smart, witty, tall, and you got a degree. I got a feeling this date could be the start of you turning it all around. Plus, you're a white man in America. You can only fall so far, ya know what I'm sayin'? Ha ha."

I can see Ernie's point, even if it's disguised in jest. I appreciate his encouragement. He's always consistent with positivity. Definitely a "glass-half-full" kind of guy. He'll make a great father someday.

"Thanks, man. I appreciate it. I hope so. I just get tired of being tossed aside. I'm just glad I got guys like you and Bob in my corner. Otherwise, this figurative ass kicking would feel a tad overwhelming. Ha."

"We got you, my man. And if all else fails, maybe I can see about throwing some work your way with my financial practice. You good with numbers?"

"For sure, I can count. A, B, C, D. You know the rest."

"Ha. Okay, well if this were an interview, I'd advise against that answer."

"Nah, it's cool, bro. I talked to Les earlier, and he mentioned something about possibly coming to work for him at his law firm. So, fingers crossed that materializes."

"Hell yeah. That'd be legit. Let me know what happens with that. And, like I said, you get desperate, just hit me up, and I'll see what I can do."

"Thanks, brother. I'll keep you in the know."

"All right. Hey, what time is it? I'm gonna have to go so you can get your shit together for this date."

I check my watch. It's 7:50 p.m. I have ten minutes to clean myself up. Gotta look my best for Holly.

"Oh, shit, yeah. It's 7:50pm. Yeah, I gotta hit the baño and clean myself up before she gets here."

"Cool. You do you, man. I'm outtie."

"All right. Later, brother."

Ernie and I shake hands and hug, each patting the other on the back. Ernie steps back following the brotherly embrace and heads for the exit. Before reaching the door, he stops in his tracks, pulls a dollar from his pocket, and puts it into the jukebox. He selects a couple of songs and presses play, before turning back to face me one last time this evening. "Hey! Something to listen to before I go."

A rhythmic keyboard begins to emanate from the pub's PA system. It's "All My Friends" by LCD Soundsystem.

Son of a bitch, I think. *That's my favorite song.*

Ernie smiles, and I return the expression. He turns away and exits the through the front door into the night. I miss my friends already.

22

It's now 7:55 p.m., and I am filling the toilet bowl of the men's room with a stream of piss. I normally would refrain from using a public restroom if at all possible, but Holly should be arriving any minute, and I'd prefer to engage her with a vacant bladder so as to limit any distractions. On a date, the few I've had as of late, I feel the need to immerse myself in the conversation—becoming enthralled with the woman's stories and thoughts and opinions on everything from love, lust, and politics to art, religion, and hate.

Their minds fascinate me, for they are much different than mine. Opposing perspectives excite me. They fuel my engine with intrigue and mystery. I relish the mystery of women. Where do they come from? What were they like prior to our meeting? How many men have they been with? Oh, all the things I do not know. I prefer never to learn the answers. Preserving them in order to keep me guessing as to what sort of past there once was. How sweet of enigmas they truly are. This practice holds my engagement long enough to stop my brain from trailing off and losing itself in reverie.

I finish pissing and notice drops of yellow-ish liquid on the toilet seat, appearing as condensation or lightly colored puddles of dew. I consider cleaning the urine off the seat with a paper towel or toilet paper, but I remember I'm inside a public men's room and have no intention of sprucing the place up. After what Bob put this lavatory through, I figure the damage has been done. This bathroom was baptized by foulness, and I don't wish to convert it to a sanitary space. At least not for free. So, I leave the piss on the seat and flush the toilet with my foot, carefully balancing on my other leg to prevent a nasty fall to the bodily fluid stained floor. I watch my watered-down urine spin and funnel to the bottom of the bowl. *Does the water actually spin counter clockwise when flushing in Australian bathrooms?* I wonder as I zip up my jeans.

I step to the sink and pump three dollops of hand soap into my palm, turn on the faucet, and wash my hands thoroughly—as if preparing for surgery like all the doctors I've seen on TV documentaries. After rinsing my hands under the faucet, I run my wet fingers through my hair, slicking the drooping follicles backward off my forehead and out of my eyes. My brownish auburn hair now looks much darker from wetness. I hope it dries soon and an appearance of greasiness dissipates.

I stare into the mirror, observing my pupils and make damn sure they aren't too dilated to notice I've been drinking all day. They look presentable. I check my swollen eye and laugh to myself as an excuse for the contusion pops into my brain like a cartoon light bulb. I splash a handful of water in my face and dry my hands with brown paper towels rolled up and stacked on the corner of the sink. I look as good as I'm gonna look. I step outside the bathroom and slowly walk to a stool at the opposite end of the bar from Dane. I'm expecting company, and privacy is required. I can catch up with him after the date or tomorrow even. I check my watch. It's 8:00 p.m. on the dot. I order a water and wait for her to arrive.

23

I've finished my glass of water and concluded standing at the bar. I take a seat in the stool near me and patiently wait for Holly's arrival. I'm no longer drunk or tipsy. I'm sobered up and equipped to operate heavy machinery. Thankfully, that's not in the cards for the evening.

Minutes pass slower and slower. The anticipation reaches a point of neuroticism and panic that I haven't felt since waiting for Santa to come down the chimney on Christmas morning when I was a boy. The main difference is Holly is real, and Saint Nick was merely a figment of my imagination propped up by my parents' Visa card.

I check my watch—8:10 p.m. She's late. I shift in my seat and attempt to ignore the tardiness. One, five, ten more minutes pass. I continue to wait. The more time that passes, the more my eczema itches. Annoying irritation grates at my skin like some form of Chinese water torture. All I want to do is scratch. Maybe if she appears, the itching will subside.

It's now 8:20pm, and Holly is late enough to warrant a text.

Me. Hey, just making sure you were still coming to hang out at Royal Tree?

I stand by for a response. It's not immediate. Maybe she's driving here and can't text back. Maybe she forgot. Maybe I'm just being stood up. Maybe she doesn't like me. Maybe she thinks I'm a loser. My brain doesn't stop concocting a number of different reasons for why Holly hasn't arrived or is failing to answer my text message. My anxiety and self-deprecation are peaking, and the struggle to remain positive is profuse. Fuck it. I'll have a drink while I wait.

"Kate, can I get a Coors Light?"

"Sure thing."

Kate swiftly removes a beer from the fridge, pops the cap off, and places the bottle in front of me at the bar. With a coaster underneath. Kate is never tardy. She's consistently punctual and more than happy to deliver a heavily poured drink or a free beer, provided you've earned it. Regardless of your relationship status at the moment, if you're a regular of the Royal Tree, Kate and the bottle stake claim as your ultimate mistresses. Johnnie Walker and Jack Daniels aren't whiskeys. They're bottom bitches for the downtrodden and thirst quenched. And they offer themselves up accordingly.

I sip at the Coors Light and think of the possible outcomes for the evening. Holly shows, we have a great time, and I see her again. Holly shows, we have a terrible time, and I never see her again. Holly doesn't show, and I get pissed wasted on Les's twenty dollars instead. The pessimist or realist in me is skeptical about my odds.

I move forward with drinking down the Coors Light. Another sip. Next is more of a guzzle. Five more minutes pass and I've finished the bottle. I check my phone for new messages and come up bupkis. It's now 8:30 p.m., and the notion I'm being stood up is settling in. I motion for Kate to supply me with more drink. She promptly delivers the cool beverage, and I ingest. My legs itch the longer I wait. I scratch harder and harder with my left foot over my right calf—to no avail. The irritation is here for the long haul. I can no longer hold back my frustration and proceed to scratch the crusty, raw skin with my fingernails. Flakes of epidermis shave off the affected area until all that's left is a red, circular pattern embedded on my right calf. An oozing follows, and beads of blood form on the area. A scab is soon to transpire, which will most assuredly itch upon development.

I pause, striving for a mechanical resolution and aim for a more internal option. So, I drink. I put my lips to the bottle and gulp down the remaining drops of beer. Nothing changes. I'm going to need something stronger.

"Kate, can I get a shot of Jameson?"

Kate grabs a fifth of Jameson and pours out a single shot. "I'll give you this one on me, but the rest are on you," she informs me, sliding the ten-ounce glass toward me.

I pick up the shot and quaff it down my esophagus. The liquor seeps through my veins after slipping into my stomach. I absorb it all. The miserable sober sensation vacates my anatomy, and a familiar drunkenness takes hold. I take in the booze and the ardor for the drink is overwhelming. *Back to status quo*, I think.

The alcohol diminishes the pain that has settled in from the constant scratching, but the itchiness remains the same—like bugs crawling across my skin or a cluster of mosquito bites festering on my leg. I attempt to ignore the annoying sensation.

Roughly thirty seconds to a minute pass by, and it's all I can bear. I scratch even harder and more furiously at the raw skin, now more of an abrasion. The pain is too severe to press on, and there's not a tube of eczema relief ointment in sight. I can think of only one other alternative. Seek and destroy. A talent I still possess. I think of my old sledgehammer from working demolition jobs and the way it would obliterate anything in its path. Time to apply a similar principle to the eczema situation.

I jump up from the barstool and push it with my ass, sliding it back away from the bar. Quickly, I stumble toward the men's room, weaving in and out of the tables and chairs aligned before me like an obstacle course. My hip bumps a couple of wooden chairs along the way, generating a loud noise as the legs glide across the hardwood floor. Kate looks toward me concerned. But my bet is she just thinks I'm a bumbling drunk at this point in the night. She's not far off.

I reach the men's room door and turn the doorknob. It's locked. What the fuck? Who the hell could be in there right now? This place is practically empty. I step back from the door and wait. A couple of minutes pass, and I can feel my skin swelling, oozing, and the isolated itching has become less specific in locale and now has turned to a collective irritation over the worn-down area. Fuck this. They've had enough time in there. I knock. No answer. I knock harder and longer. *Knock! Knock! Knock!*

"Un minuto," I hear from the other side of the door.

"Hurry up in there!"

"Un minuto! Ay dios mio!" the voice on the opposite end of the door yells.

"Vamanos!" I reply in his native tongue as I pound the door again.

I hear the toilet flush inside the bathroom, and the sink begins to run. *At least he's washing his hands*, I say to myself.

A sound vibrates the door as it's unlocked. The door flies open. It's a short Hispanic man in an apron—one of the Royal Tree cooks.

"Que demonios, cabron!" he yells at me in Spanish.

"Muevete!" I yell back in Spanish.

I step around him and enter the bathroom, slamming the door and locking it behind me. The bathroom stinks of shit. No wonder the cook was taking so long. I put my right foot up on the sink and lift my pant leg up around my knee, exposing the raw skin. The oozing has turned to full-on bleeding, having soaked the inside of my pant leg, leaving a red stain on the inseam.

I lift my shirt up over my head and remove it from my torso. I fold the shirt long ways, hot dog-style, and place it in my mouth between my teeth. Next, I reach into my front jean pocket and pull out my Bic lighter. I rub my left thumb over the top of the lighter, igniting the flame. I stare into the blaze, questioning my decision-making in this moment. I think of the old sledgehammer again. There doesn't seem to be another option.

I bite down hard on the shirt in my mouth and press the flame against my skin, burning the eczema patch. The skin singes and the pain is severe. I hold the ignited lighter up against the abraded patch for approximately three seconds. It's all the time I can muster. I feel my teeth clinch even harder, almost piercing through the cotton fabric. I let out a pain-induced growl, muffled by the shirt inserted between my teeth. The smell of burnt hair and flesh fills the bathroom, overpowering the previously existing smell of the cook's crap that had wafted about. I extinguish the flame and drop my head onto my right knee propped upon the porcelain sink. My bite releases, and heavy breathing emanates from my mouth and nostrils. I open my eyes and examine the now burned eczema patch on my calf. It's a bright red, and small bubbles of white skin have surfaced. The pain remains intense, but the itching is no more.

I drop my leg off the sink and reach for paper towels. I cover them with hand soap and soak the wad of towels under the faucet. Slowly and gently, I wipe the burned epidermal surface in an attempt to sterilize the wound. The soap stings, and I wince in response. After the cleaning, I discard of soapy paper towels into the toilet. Next, I wrap dry layers of paper towels around my calf, insulating the area. The paper sticks to my wet skin, and they should stay in place until I can remove them after returning home later in the evening. I unroll my pant leg down back around my ankle, making sure not to unwrap the homemade bandage I applied. I turn the sink back on and splash water on my face.

I look into the mirror and question the consequences of my actions and pray for no infections. The good news is I no longer am experiencing an itching sensation. The bad news is a first- or potential second-degree burn is present on my calf, which may require medical attention. Unfortunately, I am without medical insurance, so I'll have to worry about the wound later. For now, I'll return to the bar and drink the pain numb.

I exit the bathroom and return back to the bar stool I previously occupied. I don't stumble toward my seat this time. The trauma of the burn has been sobering. I rest my elbows atop the bar and run my hands over my face.

Kate approaches. "Everything come out all right in there?"

"Ha. I hope so."

"Ha. You want something to drink?"

"Yeah. I'll take a Coors Light, please."

"Sure thing."

Kate reaches into the fridge below the bar and materializes a bottle of beer with my name on it. She removes the cap and places the bottle in front of me on a coaster. I lift the bottle to my lips and take a healthy pull of beer. It's cold, and I consider pressing the bottle to my calf but choose not to do so. That would raise too many questions I'd prefer never to answer.

Suddenly, my phone vibrates. I remove the iPhone from my back pocket and check the notification. It's from "Holly Royal Tree." I check the time, and it reads 8:45 p.m. I open the message and begin to read.

HOLLY. OMG, I am so sorry! I came home from hanging out at PCM and fell asleep on my couch. Are you still at Royal Tree?

I wait a beat and contemplate how to respond. Sure, I'm upset about the tardiness, but she seems to have a valid excuse. Also, considering the depravity of my attempt to self-medicate in the bathroom only minutes ago, I don't have much room to judge. I decide to give her the benefit of the doubt.

ME. Yeah. I'm still here actually.

HOLLY: Okay. I can still come up there and meet you if you plan on staying a little longer? I could be there at 9:00 p.m.

ME. Yeah, I can stick around. 9:00 p.m. works.

HOLLY. Okay, great! I'll leave my apartment now. Sorry again.

ME. No worries. I'll see ya soon.

I put my phone down, and a slight smile runs across my face. Looks like I'll be having that date after all. The pain on my calf continues to throb, but I can suffer through. Nothing a couple of adult beverages can't take care of. I lift the bottle of beer to my lips and take a drink. I check the label. The mountains are blue.

24

It's 8:55 p.m. Planted in my stool at the bar, I sip on a Coors Light. Mountains still a shade of blue. I take it as a sign of prosperity for the future. The itching on my calf remains at bay, and the pain is dulled from the alcohol intake and a few ibuprofens obtained from Kate a little less than ten minutes ago. I told her I had a headache, and she took pity on me. Sorry about the fib, Kate. But desperation makes liars of us all.

I scan through my iPhone and type potential talking points into the notes app. I normally would just wing it on a date. But due to my peaked interest in Holly from our prior encounter, I'd like to be as prepared as possible in the event of an awkward silence where neither of us has anything to contribute in the way of conversation. I read through the talking points:

- Braves game
- Bet with Les
- Baby Baby fight
- Bob's blumpkin
- Eczema
- *High Fidelity* book

After reading through the notes, I realize 80 to 90 percent of what I've written down is ill-advised points of discussion for a first date. *What the fuck am I thinking?* I question myself. I'm sure as hell not going to open up a line of meaningful dialogue with, "So I won a gambling bet, fought an old redneck, and burned off an eczema patch, all while my friend was getting blown and shitting his brains out." I'll pass. Looks like I'll offer a recap of the Braves game and a review of Nick Hornby's *High Fidelity*. Too bad I haven't finished the book yet. At least I've seen the movie. That should suffice for cliff notes. I drink from my beer and think of highlights from the film.

I wait a few more minutes and check the time again—9:01 p.m. Any minute now. Then I hear the front door of the pub open.

I look to my left and see her standing there in the doorway. Holly. Long, curly blonde hair. Dressed in a burnt orange t-shirt with short cutoff jean shorts and sandals. She's gorgeous. Prettier than I remembered. I wave at her, trying to remain cool. She waves back and walks toward me at the bar.

I stand to greet her. "Hey," I say as I open my arms to hug her. A presumptuous move with someone I hardly know, but she returns the embrace. We take seats in the stools at the bar.

"How's it going?"

"Pretty good. Just enjoying a Saturday off work."

"Yeah, at the PCM?"

"Ha, yeah. I can't believe you've never been. Lots of great places to eat and shop there."

"Hmm. Yeah, I just haven't found the time to get down there."

"Did you just move to Atlanta or something? Trying to figure out how you could've missed the place."

"Nah, I've been here for a while now. Moved away for a bit for college, but came back after."

"Where'd you go to college?"

"University of Tulsa in Oklahoma."

"Tulsa? That's random. What brought you out there?"

"I have family out that way. Figured I'd take a stab at Midwestern life while I studied."

"How was 'Midwestern life'?"

"Flat and windy. Where'd you go to school?"

"UGA."

"Ah, in Athens?"

"Ha. Yeah that's where UGA is."

"You from Atlanta originally?"

"Yup, well, the suburbs of Atlanta. In Cumming."

"That's surprising."

"Why?"

"You don't meet a lot of native ATLiens. Everyone seems to be a transplant from one place or another."

"Yeah, well, I'm an OG, I guess. Ha. A-Town for life."

Kate approaches from behind the bar. She drops a couple *of* menus in front of us and engages.

"Hi there," Kate says.

"Hi." Holly returns the greeting.

"Anything to drink?" asks Kate.

"Yes. Could I get a Moscow Mule?" Holly orders.

"Sure thing, darling. Matt, you need anything else?" Kate inquires.

"Yes. Could I get another Coors Light?"

"Got it. Y'all gonna be eating as well?" Kate seeks to upsell us on a meal.

"I'm good on food actually, not unless you wanted something?" Holly asks me.

"Nah, I'm not hungry right now."

"Okay. Sounds good. Be right back with those drinks," Kate says, walking away to prepare our drinks.

I look at Holly and catch a glimpse of her eyes. They're dark brown and stunning—the kind a man could get lost in. Van

Morrison comes to my mind. *Could this be my brown-eyed girl?* I wonder. We'll see how the night goes.

An awkward silence settles in while we wait for our drinks. We each look around the pub and occasionally glimpse at the TV behind the bar, now playing a recap of the Braves game from earlier. Kate returns with our drinks and places them in front of us at the bar, coasters underneath each one. Holly and I raise our drinks and cheers. She sips hers from a plastic straw, and I take a slow pull from the beer.

"So … I wanted to say again how sorry I am for being super late tonight."

"It's okay. You're here now."

"Yeah, I know, but I still feel bad. I was out with my sister earlier, and we were hanging out on the PCM rooftop all day. I got home, and I guess the sun got to me and I just passed out on my couch."

"No worries. It's understandable. Though, I'll admit, I did think you were standing me up for a while there."

"No, no. I was actually looking forward to this date."

"You were?"

"Ha, yeah. I figured the conversation flowed fairly well last night, and you seemed like someone I wouldn't mind having a drink with. Plus, you were reading one of my favorite books."

"*High Fidelity*?"

"Ha, yeah, unless you had some other book with you last night. Do you always read in bars?"

"Not always. I just find it easier than reading in libraries. The silence is deafening."

"Interesting. So, how's the book?"

"*High Fidelity*?"

"Ha, well, yeah. Is there some other book you're reading right now also?"

"Ha. Nah. I'm a one-book-at-a-time man. It's good. I really like it. I feel like I identify with the main character quite a bit."

"So, does that mean you're a music snob?"

"Ha. No, not at all."

"Says the guy wearing an Arcade Fire t-shirt."

"Touché … Forgive me if I asked this last night, but have you seen the movie as well?"

"Yeah, I told you last night. It's pretty good. Have you seen the Hulu series based on it?"

"No, I haven't. Just the movie. Any good?"

"Yeah, it's told from a female perspective. The characters are essentially the same though. Just a little more modern. I actually like it better than the movie."

"Hmm, sounds cool. I'll have to check it out."

Another awkward silence settles over us. I have so much I want to tell her, but now isn't the time for talk of fights and bathroom blow jobs. I'll give her a minute to come up with a talking point while I sip my beer.

"Can I ask … what happened to your eye?" Holly questions my contusion courtesy of Baby Baby.

I laugh and desperately try to think of an excuse that isn't the truth. My first lie is forming. I hope to not make this a habit—not with her.

"Well … I was at the women's march … and there were some guys picking on a trans kid, so I got involved."

"Ha ha. You're so full of shit."

"Ha, what? Is it so hard to believe I'm a purveyor of justice? Not all heroes wear capes."

"Seriously, though. What happened?"

"I slipped and hit my head on a doorknob."

"So heroic. Who knew you were so accident prone."

"I have my moments."

We each take more pulls from our respective drinks and engage in stares at the other. I desperately search for something to say.

A compliment for Holly enters my brain, and I state the obvious. "You're really beautiful, by the way."

"Thanks. That's sweet."

"I love your hair too. Very pretty."

"Awe, thanks." Holly says, flipping her hair off her shoulder.

My heart flutters. I can't believe this gorgeous creature is indulging me. I feel my guard lower and a sense of vulnerability is instilled. "You're welcome. It's easy to state the facts."

"Ha, whatever. You're just trying to earn brownie points."

"How am I scoring?"

"You have a good lead thus far."

I smile and take another drink of beer. I sit up farther in my stool and lean in closer to Holly. Not an intrusive distance, but just far enough away that she could hear a whisper if I chose. I feel on top of my game. The level of alcohol I've ingested up to this point has me well lubricated and confident enough to guide the conversation, minus any hindrance of belligerence or sloppiness. Plus, the vulnerability I'm feeling is making me more willing and honest. No games or facades. Unintentionally, I've taken Ernie's advice and I'm "being myself."

"It's really nice out tonight."

"Yeah, it is. I wouldn't mind sitting outside, if you're okay with that?"

"Sure, that works for me."

"Will they serve us outside?"

"Yeah, Kate will come out and check on us here and there."

"Okay. Sounds good. Ready when you are."

We stand up from our stools, grab our drinks, and make our way to the front patio outside. I follow behind Holly and glance at her butt and legs as she moves for the front door. She's flawless. I can tell she must've been an athlete at some point in her younger days.

As we pass Dane at the end of the bar, he looks up at me and grins, offering a thumbs-up as we pass. I silently laugh and continue following Holly out the front door. We reach an open high-top table and take a seat. It's comfortably warm, maybe 80 degrees Fahrenheit, and the stars are visible above. The perfectness of the evening is alarming, and I can't help but feel fear. Fear that all this good luck will come screeching to a halt at any moment. Instead of indulging in the panic, I take a sip of beer and take the ride.

25

We talked and talked more outside. The conversation flowed smoothly without disruption, like Guinness from the tap. I became lost in her stories, our banter, her looks, and I couldn't take my eyes off of her. The only moments I'd catch myself losing focus of the conversation were the times I'd lose myself in a daydream about kissing her, touching her, getting my hands tangled in her hair. I'd daydream of days, weeks, months, and years down the line, together with her. A future seemed plausible. And then the fear of it all going away in an instant would present itself, snapping me back into the present, grasping at keywords to realign myself with whatever she was speaking of at the time.

I learned many things about her. She was a nurse, recently graduated and had just completed her residency. She liked the same bands as me. She preferred *Seinfeld* to *Friends*. She was a former competitive cheerleader in high school, which explained her athletic legs. And she loved to drink.

My heart skipped a beat after Kate brought us another round of drinks and, upon asking her how her Moscow Mule tasted, Holly responded with, "Alcohol is life." A laughable comment, but one that struck a chord with me, and I couldn't help but relate. I was officially strapped in for takeoff at this time.

"I feel like you know enough about me. What about you? What do you do?"

"Well, up until recently, I worked in demolition at a produce warehouse."

"Interesting. So, you don't work there anymore?"

"Nah, I gave it up. Felt like it was time for something less labor intensive."

"So, what have you been up since you left?"

"Odd jobs mostly. Interviewing at a number of places. It looks like I could be going to work at a law firm soon though."

"Really? Well that sounds like a step up. Pay wise."

"Yeah, a friend of mine is an attorney. He said he had something for me, and we'd connect soon about it."

"What would you be doing there?"

"Not sure yet. Probably legal aid shit."

"Hmm, well, at least you have a plan. Helps to know people, I guess."

"Yeah, he's a good guy. I wouldn't mind working for him. It'd be nice to put those old college credits to good use."

"What did you study?"

"Human resources. So, I know just enough to not get fired for being an asshole."

"That's good. As long as you can apply it."

"Ha ha. Easier said than done sometimes."

We break in the conversation and return to our drinks. She lets me try her Moscow Mule, and I let her have a turn with my Coors Light. I feel my phone vibrating in my pocket, but I ignore it. Most likely it's Bob messaging me and looking for an update or asking about how to get stains out of clothing. I can touch base with him later. But for now, I'm too wrapped up in Holly to divert my attention elsewhere.

"So, how'd the Braves game turn out?"

"They pulled off the win late in the game."

"Oh, nice. Go Bravos!"

"Yeah, it was great game. Plus, I won twenty bucks too." I let the news about the wager with Les slip.

"Oh yeah? Well congratulations on that. Do you bet on sports often?"

"Not really. Only when I know I can win."

"And what made you think you'd win this time?"

"A hunch."

"That doesn't sound very scientific."

"Well then let's just say I had a hypothesis that needed testing. How's that for scientific?"

"Better. I've never gambled much. Mostly just blackjack when I'm in Vegas."

"You go there often?"

"No, just been a couple times. Bachelorette weekends. Have you ever been?"

"Once. That was enough for me."

"You not a Vegas fan?"

"I find it kinda tacky and gauche. Mostly filled with losers trying to win big on a fixed game."

"And how is betting on sports any different?"

"I understand the matchups with sports. There's statistics involved. And I enjoy the thrill of being relatively out of control of the outcome."

"There's statistics involved in blackjack."

"But not the kind I can understand. I guess you could say I'm not great with math. Ha. I prefer to size up opponents based on physical matchups. It's easier for me to gauge."

"So how do you size me up?"

"Ha. I think I could take you."

"Think again, slick. I take kickboxing classes after work. I'm not sure you could withstand my roundhouse kicks."

"Ha. Oh yeah? I guess I stand corrected."

"Yeah, and don't forget that." Holly returns a flirtatious smile.

We return to sipping our drinks. She finishes her Moscow Mule, and I down the remainder of my Coors Light. This particular beer tastes more satisfying than any other beer I've ever tasted. Even more so than the first beer after a long day of manual labor. The mountains of the bottle have remained blue the entire time. Must be a good sign.

"Do you want another drink?"

"Yes, please."

"Okay. I'll go inside and order them so we don't have to wait. You good with holding down the fort?"

"Affirmative." Holly salutes me sarcastically.

"At ease, soldier. I'll be right back."

I pick up the empty copper mug and bottle of beer and return to the inside of the pub. I order another round from Kate and take a look toward Dane, sitting to my left. He drinks his scotch and water with the straw bent over the glass and gives me a look with his eyebrows raised high. Kate delivers the drinks, and they engage.

"How's the date going?" asks Dane.

"Great so far. She's a cool chick."

"Cute too," Dane adds.

"Yeah, like a young Julia Roberts or Kyra Sedgewick."

"I can see that," Dane replies.

"She on your tab tonight?" asks Kate.

"Yeah, just put her drinks on my tab, and I'll settle up later."

"Gotcha. Well, have fun out there," Kate says.

"I'll do my best."

"Hey, before you go, does she have a friend for me?" asks Dane jokingly.

"Ha. I'll do some digging and get back to you on that."

Dane and Kate laugh, and I pick up the drinks and head for the door. Before I turn around, the pessimist in me worries she won't be there when I return. I reach the entryway and look through the door. She's still there. Holding down the fort as promised. And she's even checking her makeup in a compact mirror. My neurosis is now at ease.

26

Holly and I continue our banter outside. We discuss politics and religion—two topics I've always heard not to engage in in public. Though I've tended not to heed that advice. Besides, she's the one who brought politics and religion up in the conversation. Seems appropriate given it's an election year and, according to evangelicals, Jesus could come back at any minute. I reject that hypothesis, but in the event Jesus does return, I expect the first round of drinks to be on him. I'll bring the water.

"So, do you know who you're voting for?" asks Holly.

"Not yet. You?"

"I don't vote."

"Why not?"

"Seems like a waste of time. We live in Georgia. This state always votes Republican."

"True, but it's only a waste then if you vote Democrat."

"Which is why I won't vote. If I were to vote, I'd cast a ballot for the liberal."

"You consider yourself a liberal?"

"Not per se. More of a libertarian. What about you? Liberal or conservative?"

"Neither. I'm a registered Independent. So, I guess you could say I could go either way. Depending on who's buying."

"Fair enough. So long as you're socially liberal."

"I like to think of myself as radically social liberal. I have no room to judge."

"So why aren't you a Democrat?"

"I don't like labels."

"Funny."

We each take pulls from our drinks and look up at the night sky. The moon and stars illuminate the darkness. I used to ponder if there was something more than wasting away in bars and at jobs we hate for money that's not enough. Somewhere along the way, I lost that sense of wonderment—perhaps after losing friends and family members too early in my teens and twenties. Trauma as such can take a toll on a person. Ideological creeds and superstitions find themselves obsolete afterward. After tonight, though, Holly may reinvigorate my willingness to believe in otherworldly possibilities.

"Did you grow up religious at all?"

"Yes, actually. Irish Catholic."

"Catholic? Interesting."

"Ha. How so?"

"Well, I just never figured a Catholic for being socially liberal."

"We're not all raised with fire and brimstone. Besides, I was always more of a cafeteria catholic."

"Ha. What's a 'cafeteria catholic'?"

"Ha, it's just a nice way of saying someone who picks and chooses what they want to follow—like a dogma buffet," I explain. "What about you? Raised religious or no?"

"Yeah, sorta. Grew up going to Baptist churches, but I don't really go much anymore. Except for Easter and Christmas. For me, it's kinda like the Olympics. I normally could care less about swimming or curling, but every four years, I give it a chance."

"Ha. I like that analogy. Gold medalists are like Jesus. We

don't pay him much attention, except for when the whole world is watching."

"Amen."

"Peace be with you," I say, making the sign of an invisible cross with my hand.

We laugh and return to our drinks. My mind wonders where the next Olympics will occur and which anointed athletic American deity will appear on a Wheaties box.

I gulp down more my beer and stare into Holly's eyes. Her pupils could restore a man's belief in God. For how else would one explain her existence? Though her tempting appeal could also be the devil's work. The persuasion to bite the apple is overwhelming. So, I refrain and guzzle the beer instead.

Soon after, a homeless person walks up to us on the patio. She's a black woman in her midthirties, with a bandana wrapped around her head, pushing back her unkempt kinky hair. A dirty, worn sleeveless "Atlanta Falcons Super Bowl LI Champions" shirt covers her torso. Given the fact Atlanta lost the Super Bowl that year, she must've bought the shirt from Goodwill or the same place refugees in third world countries obtain America's discarded outerwear. The oddity of her appearance is a long, sunflower patterned skirt sitting high on her waist, which, from the shape it's in, appears to be new. Not a stain or wrinkle in sight. She must've scrounged together a few bucks and treated herself to something nice recently. We all deserve to treat ourselves now and again.

The homeless woman stumbles toward Holly and me. "Have any change to spare?" she asks.

"No."

"Sorry. I just have a credit card," Holly adds.

"Can you buy me a beer, then?" the homeless woman retorts.

"You can have the rest of mine," I say, offering the last half of my Coors Light to her.

"That works." The homeless woman accepts.

I hand her the remainder of my bottle of Coors Light, and she swiftly takes it from my grasp as I recoil my hand the way one does when feeding a treat to a hungry animal. She puts her lips on the rim of the bottle and tilts it straight up, chugging the beer down in a matter of seconds. After finishing off the longneck, she attempts to hand the empty bottle back to me, as if I'm a catering server.

"That's all you," I say, throwing up my hands, wanting nothing to do with the empty bottle.

"A'ight, then," says the homeless woman, before tipping the bottle back up and draining the last drops of beer from the container.

The homeless woman drops her arms to her side and releases the bottle from her hand, letting it fall to the pavement, like a discarded candy wrapper in a movie theater. She pulls her arm up and beats her fist on her chest 1 time, cocks her head upward, and loudly burps into the sky. Holly and I curl our faces in disgust. I place my hand over my mouth, while Holly places her hand over the top of her Moscow Mule, attempting to prevent any of the homeless woman's gastrointestinal particles from trickling down into her mug. Just as quickly as she chugged half a beer, she equally as quickly turns away and wanders into the Royal Tree, leaving Holly and I alone to process the interaction.

"I don't wanna sound insensitive, but that was really gross," Holly says.

"Yeah, that actually kinda pissed me off. Was burping right in front of us necessary?"

"Maybe she's mentally ill."

"Maybe. I wonder who she's voting for?"

"I'm assuming not the Green Party."

Holly has punched up my joke, and I am pleased. I think about the homeless woman and how sorry I feel for her. She's obviously down on her luck and desperate for money and drink. I can't help but relate. Unwanted empathy on my part. I hope to never feel this way again.

27

My thirst is quenched, and I am without drink as we sit outside on the patio. The pain from burning my eczema earlier has dulled, and the booze is most assuredly a contributing factor. Though the pain is diminished, it still remains present. It's the only thing grounding me in reality and not assuming this encounter with the mesmerizingly beautiful Holly is not a dream. If the discomfort were more severe, I'd assume a hallucination. If that were the case, I'd revel in the ride until the magic wore off.

I check the time. It's 10:00 p.m. I could use something stronger than a beer. I look to Holly and notice her mug is empty as well. Best act as a good host and ask her if she'd appreciate a refill.

"I was gonna go inside for another drink. Want me to bring you something?"

"Sure. I don't like to mix liquors, so I think I'll stick with vodka."

"Alrighty. Anything in particular?"

"Hmm … How about … a vodka tonic?"

"Cool. I'll be right back with your order."

I bow to Holly as if I'm "Jeeves the butler" and backpedal toward the Royal Tree entrance. I turn, facing the glass paned front door, and enter. The pub is essentially empty, with the exception of Dane, plus Kate behind the bar, and the homeless woman. I walk inside and put a dollar in the jukebox. I skim through possible tracks and wind up selecting "Georgia" by Ray Charles and "Brown Eyed Girl" by Van Morrison. Fitting ditties for Holly.

I'm buzzed or tipsy, however one wants to put it, and feel it's a decent time to put the next foot forward and test the waters of drunkenness for another time today. I feel I'm ahead in the game with Holly, and she seems to respond to every pitch I throw her way, like a veteran batter with a .300 average. All I have to do is treat this like a home run derby and play the pitching coach the whole way through. Eventually, we could both win the contest together.

I lean against the bar, next to Dane and signal to Kate it's time for another order of drinks. She sees me and holds up a single fore-finger, letting me know to wait one moment. She's busy dealing with the homeless woman, now staggering at the lip of the bar, desperately trying to order a beer with whatever change she has on her person. From the looks of the way she's sparingly counting out nickels and dimes, it seems like she'll have just enough for a Coke or a splash of draft.

"How much you got here?" asks Kate.

"Five, ten, fifteen, twenty, twenty-five, thirty-five, forty-five, fifty-five. Oh, there's a quarter—seventy, seventy-five, eighty-five, ninety-five, one-oh-five. How much is that?" asks the homeless woman.

"That's $1.05. The cheapest beer we have right now is $3."

"So, what can I get with that?"

"Nothing. I can either give you a water or a coke."

"Come on now. You can't spare nothin'?"

"Sorry. Those are the prices."

"Ah, shit! Come on now! I'm thirsty!"

"I can give you a water if you're thirsty, free of charge."

"That ain't what I want though!"

"Then you're gonna need to come up with a couple more dollars or I can't serve you."

"Ah damn, come on! This is bullshit. Just give me something to drank. Y'all don't have any money?" the homeless woman directs toward Dane and I.

"I'm paying with a card." Dane says.

"What 'bout you? I saw you put dollars in that jukebox!"

"I got money, but none for you," I respond.

"You heartless bastards!"

"Look, you need to stop yelling at customers, or I'm going to have to ask you to leave," Kate interjects.

I look to Dane, and he shakes his head. He doesn't appear to have any interest in getting involved in the situation. I, personally, am tired of listening to the noise and having a homeless woman with less than two dollars to her name hold up my drink order. Like her, I too am thirsty, and I'm ready to return to my date.

"Kate, look. Give her a beer. Put it on my tab. But make sure it's a cheap beer. And I'll also take a double Bulleit on the rocks and a vodka tonic."

"You sure, Matt?" asks Kate.

"Yeah, let's just speed this process up."

"If you're cool with that, then I am too," Kate answers.

"Yeah, let's just keep rolling."

"You good with a Coors Light?" Kate asks the homeless woman.

"Yeah. Coors. I can do that," responds the homeless woman.

"Just make sure you leave the change for her as a tip," I tell the homeless woman.

"Yeah, yeah," grumbles the homeless woman.

Kate reaches for the fridge under the bar and pulls out a Coors Light longneck. She uncaps the top and sits the bottle on the bar in front of the homeless woman. No coaster underneath. I guess she figures she wouldn't use it anyhow. Next, she pours mine and Holly's drinks and delivers those to me. The homeless woman picks up the bottle of beer and chugs it the same way she did outside, minutes earlier. She doesn't stop until every last drop is down her gullet, like a seagull swallowing fish at sea. Upon downing the beer, she displaces the bottle on top of the bar resting on its side and burps loudly again. Dane and I laugh at her belch, as Dane covers his glass with his hand, similar to how Holly had done outside.

"Can I get another?" the homeless woman asks of me.

"No, that's enough."

"Come on now! I know you got the money!"

"That's not the point."

"Well shit! Fuck you then!"

"I'd prefer a thank you."

"Forget you!"

"I can't wait."

"Look, he bought you a beer. That's it. If you don't have anymore money, I'm going to have to ask you to leave," Kate tells her.

"Bitch, I didn't wanna drink in this trap anyhow!" yells the homeless woman.

"Oh, I'm a bitch? I'll show you just how bitchy I am. Get out of my bar!" Kate raises her voice.

"Oh, you kickin' me out now?"

"Yeah, leave and don't come back!" demands Kate.

"Fine! I'm gonna leave. And y'all can fuck off straight to hell!" the homeless woman damns us.

The homeless woman gathers the change she had previously sprawled out on the bar top and storms away. She heads for the door in a fuss. As she leaves the pub, she throws up a middle finger in Dane, Kate, and my general direction.

"You forgot to leave a tip," I remind her as the door closes behind her.

"What the fuck just happened? Ha ha." Dane laughs, questioning what recently transpired.

"Another glorious day at the Tree," Kate adds.

"Thanks, Kate. I'm gonna take these back outside."

"Sure thing, honey. Just don't go feeding anymore stray cats," Kate says.

"Ha. Understood."

I gather Holly and my drinks and walk toward the patio. I push the front door open with my foot and exit toward outside. Before I fully exit the indoor pub area, I hear the homeless woman screaming obscenities. They're clearly directed at Kate. I can tell by the gratuitous use of the slurs "cunt" and "bitch." Though I have checked myself while being rather cunty at times in the past, so who knows. There could be insults directed at me as well. Holly sits in place, and a stunned look appears across her face. It's apparent she is vastly caught off guard, especially considering she was not present inside the pub less than a minute ago.

"Hey, Kate. This lady is losing her shit out here. You may wanna come out."

Kate paces out from behind the bar and makes haste for the front door. I fully exit the pub for the patio, and Kate and Dane follow behind. I place the drinks on the high top in front of Holly. We connect eyes, and Holly mouths to me, "What the fuck?"

I nervously smile and focus back on the belligerent homeless woman on the patio.

"Fuck you, muthafuckas! I don't need yo shit!" the homeless woman screams.

"Get outta here, or I'm gonna call the cops!" Kate says forcefully.

"Eat my pussy, bitch!" the homeless woman harkens back.

"Dane, call the cops!" Kate directs Dane.

Dane fumbles for his cell phone. He removes the phone from his fleece pocket and hesitantly dials 9-1-1. He has yet to press the call button and holds the phone in the air.

"I have the police ready to come. If you leave now, I won't dial them," Dane says, attempting to reason with the woman.

"Fuck the po-po! And fuck you bitches!" yells the homeless woman once more.

"Just get the hell outta here! Now!" Kate demands authoritatively.

"Fine! Fine! You cunt ass bitch!" says the homeless woman as she begins to turn and leave the patio area.

Dane, Kate, Holly, and I breathe a sigh of relief as the homeless woman walks away. Our edginess settles as the situation becomes more manageable, and I look to Holly, concerned this altercation may signal the end of an otherwise great first date. The homeless woman stumbles roughly three feet off the patio before turning around and waddling back toward the outdoor seating area.

"'Fore I go, I'ma leave yo bitch ass sumethin to clean up!" informs the homeless woman.

As the homeless woman completes her sentence, she turns her back to the pub's front window, bends over, and lifts her skirt up over her back. Suddenly, a stream of piss sprays out from her behind her rear, laminating the entire pub window with urine. The stream seems to last five to ten seconds, if not forever. Dane, Holly, Kate, and I step back in retreat, jaws dropped in horror and disbelief at what we are witnessing.

"What the fuck?" yells a shocked Kate.

Eventually, the stream turns to dribbles, running down the back of the homeless woman's legs. She drops her skirt and stands back upright. Finally, she's empty.

"Holy. Shit," Dane says, still in disbelief.

"Yeah! Now, you deal with that, muthafuckas!" says the homeless woman as she stumbles away toward the MARTA train station at the opposite end of the strip mall parking lot.

After the homeless woman has officially left the premises, we each look to the other for confirmation of what we just saw. Judging by the looks on our faces, we're all in agreement. Not to mention the urine running down the pub window like water after a car wax application.

"Jesus titty fucking Christ. Sorry you had to see that," Kate tells us, before walking back inside to the pub.

"You still want me to call the police?" asks Dane.

"No, it's a little late for that now," Kate says.

Dane and Kate reenter the pub. I look to Holly, and her eyes are wide open in astonishment and amazement. I can tell she's never witnessed anything so intense. In all honesty, neither have I. Another thing we have in common. I grab our drinks and pick them back up off the high top.

"You wanna go back inside?"

"Please."

Holly rises from her chair, and we return to the pub. We sit a few chairs down from Dane and reminisce with Kate and him about what just happened.

"How the hell did that get started?" asks Holly.

"I kicked her out after she kept hassling Matt for beer money," Kate answers.

"And that's how she responded?" asks Holly.

"Yeah! And I still can't believe she was able to pee like that on command in front of people!" Dane says with bewilderment.

"Fucking nutjob. Now I'm gonna have to clean that up later." Kate adds.

"God, I'm sorry. That's disgusting. That's easily the most disturbing thing I've ever seen," Holly informs us.

"It's up there," Kate admits.

Kate pours each one of us a shot of Jameson and toasts Dane, Holly, and me for sticking around after urine-gate. A magnanimous gesture on Kate's part. We raise our shot glasses and cheers to "an interesting night." Dane, Kate, Holly, and I swallow our drinks simultaneously, smirk, and return to our own business. Van Morrison's "Brown Eyed Girl" plays over the pub PA system.

"I played this for you," I tell Holly.

"Ha, thanks. I'm guessing I'm the 'brown eyed girl'?

"Definitely."

We each partake in our drinks, even more so, as we listen to Van Morrison sing his classic chorus. I smile at Holly, and she smiles back. And the music plays.

28

Holly and I sit at the bar, engaging in a two-way conversation. Dane and Kate are interacting and making minimal chitchat. I ask Holly if I can try her vodka tonic. I haven't drunk one of those in about ten years, and after tasting the drink, I instantly am reminded why I gave them up. To be fair, though, I've never been a fan of mixers in my liquor. Holly asks to try my bourbon on the rocks, and I oblige. She takes a drink and immediately passes the glass of bourbon back to me. Her face curls and contorts, rejecting the dark liquor.

"Not a whiskey girl?"

"Not at all."

I raise the glass to my lips and take a long, slow drink of bourbon. Almost as if I need confirmation that I still fancy the liquor, despite Holly's lack of endorsement. My long-standing assessment is confirmed. I love it. The bourbon offers a soothing burn as it runs down my throat into my stomach. I feel drunk, but I'm still managing to keep my composure. It helps that Holly appears moderately inebriated as well. Needless to say, both of our egos are dying a slow death in the late hours, and a lack of any judgment or facades are fading.

The bar becomes silence as Dane and Kate and Holly and I

take a break from conversation. The jukebox hasn't churned out a tune in some minutes, and at this juncture, it's a matter that needs immediate addressing. Holly plays with her curls, twisting them around her right forefinger and releasing them. Her curls bounce back into formation, only now somewhat tighter than before the manipulation. I worry she's becoming either tired or bored. I decide to liven the atmosphere.

"Do you wanna play songs on the jukebox?"

"Sure. We can do that."

"What would you like to hear?"

"What songs do they have?"

"This thing can pull up any song you can think of, though I prefer the classic jukeboxes with fixed albums myself.

"Very analog of you … Hmm, well I have a couple in mind. I don't have any cash though. Just a debit card."

"I got a few bucks. Here ya go. Knock yourself out." I say, handing Holly a dollar.

"Thanks. Be right back."

Holly rises to her feet, turns, and approaches the jukebox. Dollar in hand. I watch her as she walks away. I admire her figure and the way she moves. She appears to glide across the pub floor. Slowly, yet with an impatience to play her songs. She stands facing the digital jukebox screen and inserts the dollar before scanning the endless number of tracks.

I'm interested to hear her selections. As she peruses the song selections, she pulls her hair over to one side of her shoulder and returns to curling her locks around her fingers. I can see the back of her neck. It's long and slender. And I can imagine myself nuzzling my face between her jugular and collarbone. Kissing ever so delicately. Her ass looks particularly supple in her cutoff shorts and connects to her long, athletic legs. Oh, those legs. I'd love to have those thighs and calves sprawled out across my lap as I comfortably scratch and tickle them until goosebumps arise upon her skin. In due time, I hope.

Holly concludes playing jukebox DJ and turns back, facing me at the bar. Loudly, Whitney Houston's "I Wanna Dance with Somebody" plays over the PA system. The opening drum beat and bass line is instantly recognizable, and I laugh at the choice. She laughs as well and lip-synchs the lyrics as she strolls back to her bar stool.

"Interesting choice for a gin joint like this."

"Well you gotta play Whitney at some point in the night."

"I have no problem with Whitney. Just an interesting setting for her to make an appearance."

"Just paying my respects."

Holly continues to mouth the lyrics. Eventually, the lip-synching turns to actual audible singing on Holly's part. I take notice of her singing voice. It's imperfect, but I love the enthusiasm she has for the track. I look over Holly's shoulder and notice Kate singing along as well. Dane is nonplussed and can only smile at the occurrence. Not to be left out, I chime in as well, belting out my own mediocre baritone version of the hit single from yesteryears. Levity has filled the room and awakened the remaining few.

"Do you wanna dance?"

"What?" she asks trying to hear over the music.

"Do you wanna dance?" I say louder.

"Ha. I'm not a big dancer."

"Ha, me neither. But I can do this," I say as I begin to bounce my shoulders with the beat of song, in a quasi-planted shoulder dance.

Holly laughs at my moves. I can tell I'm in a full state of intoxication due to the fact I'm even attempting to dance, much less in this fashion. It's not normally my style to entertain others, but Holly seems to enjoy my attempt and takes my shoulder flaring for a joke. Soon, I feel like a circus seal dancing for the amusement of strangers and consider pausing. And then I see the amusement on Holly's face and press forward for her pleasure. For the first time in years, it feels like I'm unselfishly making someone else happy. The realization is sobering, and I pause making a fool of myself and take another sip of bourbon. The drink helps straighten me out. I'll let Holly finish singing the song herself, with Kate on backup vocals.

The song ends after almost five minutes and numerous repeated choruses. Kate offers Holly and me a short applause, and we bow our heads in thanks. Holly drinks more of her vodka tonic, and I join in with my bourbon.

Dane looks up from his watered-down scotch to address the room. "I thought a flash mob was going to break out over there at one point! Ha ha." He laughs.

"That'll be a cold day in hell, Dane."

"I don't know. Could be sooner than you think. It's feeling a little chilly in here," Dane jokes.

"Well, I'd suggest zipping up that fleece a bit farther then."

Dane laughs and returns to bending his straw over the back of his glass and sucking away at his scotch and water. There's a brief pause in the music, while the next song queues up in the playlist. Holly and I connect eyes, if only for a second, though the moment lasts a millennium. The moment passes, and Holly leans in closer.

"Do you like the Talking Heads?"

"Yeah, I love the Talking Heads. Why?"

"I think you'll like the next song."

"What is it?"

"The Lumineers."

"What do The Lumineers have to do with the Talking Heads?"

"You'll see."

The song begins. A familiar guitar riff is played. It's acoustic but familiar nonetheless.

I recognize the lyrics. It's a cover of Talking Heads' "This Must Be the Place." I've never heard this version, and my ears perk up in interest. My intrigue in Holly heightens, as the original version was one of my favorite songs growing up. A comforting warmth blankets my skin, and never have the lyrics sounded more poignant. A surge of sentimentality rushes my senses, and I'm reminded of earlier days, and a brighter future appears along the horizon.

I watch as Holly mouths the words to the song and can't help but truly smile with happiness—an unfamiliar emotion for some time. I have no idea how it will last, but for the next four minutes, I'll relish every second.

29

It's now 11 p.m. The drinks are flowing, and Holly and I are taking turns playing songs on the jukebox. It's turned into a game—each of us attempting to outdo the other on quality track listings. Holly took an early lead with Whitney Houston and the Lumineers cover of the Talking Heads. I counter with "All I Want" by LCD Soundsystem and "12:51" by The Strokes. Not one to be denied, she selects "I Need My Girl" by The National and "Want You Back" by Haim. As a hail Mary pass, I queue up Joan Jett's cover of "Crimson and Clover," followed by "Spitting Venom" by Modest Mouse. Holly doesn't play another song on the jukebox but still lands a knockout punch when she informs me of her love for the Modest Mouse track. My favorite song from my favorite band. *How could this all be going so well?* I think to myself in pleasant disbelief.

At this point, I couldn't be more attracted to her. I was sold hours ago, but now I'm willing to buy stock. I've never been a fan of labels, but for every hipster, a self-sufficient woman with impeccable musical taste is a living, breathing wet dream. I've held strong for most of the night, but I can no longer contain my level of attraction. I desperately desire to make a move. I want to lean in and kiss her and allow my hands to tangle in her curly golden locks of hair. I want our primal urges to take hold and devour each other in a sea of ecstasy. I know I've preferred mystery in the past, but now I'm desperate for answers. I have to know where I stand with her. "What's the story, morning glory?" as the band Oasis once said.

"So, I have to ask … And forgive me if this is none of my business, but I have to know … Are you seeing anyone else right now?" I struggle drunkenly to choose my words.

"Ha, why? Are you the jealous type?"

"Yes … Sorry, but I am … I just … I just really like you. And … I wanted to know if you were having a good time … is all." I sound like a Christopher Walken character.

"Ha. Yeah, I'm having a good time." Holly smiles. "And I like you too."

I reach out and put Holly's hand in mine. This is the first time we've touched since the initial hug earlier in the night. Her hand is small and delicate, dwarfed in mine. Her palms are soft and well maintained, whereas mine are worn, bent, and busted from years of manual labor. I look down at our appendages intertwined and rub my thumb over the top of her hand. I lift my head and look into her eyes. I want to kiss her, and I feel she wants me to do so as well. This is a perfect moment to do so, but I fall victim to cowardice and hold off. I hate myself in the seconds after, like when a car passes you on the highway only to make you realize you're driving too slowly in the left-hand lane.

"Are you seeing anyone else, though?"

"To be honest … there is one other guy."

"Oh … Is he as tall as me?"

"Ha. What? I mean … no. He isn't actually."

"Ha, well I guess I got that going for me."

"Ha, yeah. But … I'm beginning to lose interest in him."

"Since when?"

"For about a week now."

"Well, I'm not seeing anybody."

"Are you saying, you only want to date me?"

"That's what I'm getting at."

"It seems a little sudden to make commitments, but … I wouldn't have a problem with that."

"Does that mean you're gonna dump the other guy, then?"

"We'll have to see."

"That's fair. I just want you to know … I can wait. Ha. I've been waiting."

"Waiting for what?"

"The right thing."

And with that, I let go of her hand. We each pick up our drinks and polish them off. I finish mine first and wait for her to down the vodka tonic combo. She does so like a champ. I check the time, and it's now a quarter till midnight. Holly yawns and it's clear she's tired.

"I'm getting pretty sleepy."

"Yeah, it might be about that time. You didn't drive, did you?" I make sure she's safe to get home.

"No. I took an Uber."

"Okay. Good. Want to make sure you get home safe."

"That's sweet."

"You gonna call the Uber now?"

"Yeah, I'm doing that now." Holly informs me as she opens the Uber app on her phone and orders the car to pick her up.

"How long till it's here?"

"Five minutes."

"Okay, well, we can go outside and wait on it."

"Okay. Sounds good."

I look to Kate and inform her that we're going to step outside, and I'll be back in a few minutes. Kate nods in acknowledgment. Holly gathers her purse as I stand from the stool, hoping not to stumble. My legs are a tad wobbly, and balance is not my friend. I worry gravity will take over and send me collapsing to the floor. But I'm able to gather my wits. And for the first time in hours, I focus on the dulled burning pain on my calf. It helps stabilize my body and mind. We walk to toward the front door. I follow behind Holly and take in the sights of her moving across the bar floor once more before she leaves for the night or for good. I'm uncertain if my request for monogamy came across as too controlling or desperate.

Holly slides down the bar and waves goodbye to Dane and Kate and tells them she had a good time. They return the sentiment. Even after countless drinks, she still moves as fluid as water passing through a dam. A tidal wave of sex, intrigue, power, and intelligence. Hurricane Holly. Her aura and presence bulldozed me, and my edges have smoothed. A passing encounter? I didn't stand a chance.

30

Holly and I stand outside on the sidewalk, away from the patio of the Royal Tree. We're waiting on her Uber to arrive, which is now late by a couple of minutes. Not a shock given it's a Saturday night. We stand beside each other and don't say a word for roughly a minute before I decide to break the silence.

"I had a great time tonight."

"Yeah, me too. Thanks for overlooking my tardiness."

"Ha, no problem. I was glad you were actually able to make it out."

"Well, I'm glad you agreed to wait."

"So am I."

We pause the conversation. I look into her dark brown eyes. Her pupils are angled upward toward mine. *It's now or never*, I think. I step forward and my diaphragm is now leveled with her breasts and only a few inches apart. I don't even contemplate the potential of her rejecting my advance. Too many indicators and signals were received throughout the night to second-guess a move for intimacy. I lift my hands and place them on her hips. She looks down and then gazes back up toward my face, now inching in closer for a first kiss. The moment of truth. How will she respond? I see her eyes close as she leans her face closer to mine. Our lips connect and contract over each other's. Not one time, but many. I pull her in closer until our bodies are fully against one another's. Room for the Holy Ghost be damned.

The embrace intensifies with each kiss. A peck of the lips would have satisfied, but expectations are exceeded and deep, passionate, drunken kisses are exchanged. No awkwardness, no fumbling, no struggles to decide whose head is placed or turned in whichever direction. We're completely in synch. As if we've done this dance before.

We cease the intense make-out session for a moment to breathe. Our foreheads rest against each other's and the ends of our noses touch. We maintain eye contact. Not a word is spoken. We break our gazes and look around the strip mall parking lot to make sure no one is around to witness our connection. No one is around with the exception of some moviegoers exiting a cinema approximately twenty yards away.

The kissing resumes, beginning first as soft and delicate before metamorphosing into a more French form. I feel her tongue caress mine as I hold her tight. Her breasts are smashed against my torso, and my body responds in return. I'm at full attention and the desire intensifies. Elation overtakes my senses and completely numbs the pain emanating from the burn on my leg. A natural cortisone.

I wish we were some place more private than a suburban parking lot, but such is life. I feel her fingers grip the belt loops on my jeans and I kiss her deeper in response. I don't want this experience to end. Happiness hasn't been easy to come by of recent. At least not the kind found outside of a bottle. It's a foreign concept about which I am now growing eager to learn.

Just as our temperatures rise, the Uber arrives. A black Honda Civic with a white Uber logo stuck to the corner of the windshield. As the car pulls up to the curb, Holly and I release our grips on each other and step back a foot. The window of the Honda Civic rolls down, and the driver calls out "Holly?"

Holly waves at him, and I open the back passenger side door for her.

"Well, I guess get home safe."

"Will do. Assuming the driver isn't a murderer."

"Ha ha. In that case, keep me on speed dial until you get home."

"Screw that. I'll put the police on speed dial."

"Ha ha. Good call. Okay, well, have a good rest of your night."

"You too."

Holly and I kiss one last time before she climbs into the back of the Uber.

"I'll text you tomorrow," I let her know.

"Alrighty. I'll look forward to that."

"Ha. Goodnight."

"Night."

I close her door, and the Uber pulls away from the curb and drives away from the Royal Tree. Off it goes into the night, carrying the most intriguing woman I've had the privilege to share drinks with. Consistent nights at the Royal Tree had paid off. For without that endurance and pub loyalty, I may never have met the lovely Holly. And again, more Talking Heads lyrics pop into my head, which, this time, I sing out loud.

I stroll back to the patio and lean against a high top, taking in the evening. I check the time. It's midnight, and I could use a celebratory drink. Maybe even a shot. Or both. I'll see if Dane would like to join me.

31

Returning into the pub, I scan the bar area. Dane remains planted in his stool and Kate is behind the bar changing the channels on the TV, looking for some form of entertainment on her long, slow night. I select the barstool to Dane's right and sit down.

Dane turns to me and raises his eyebrows, expecting a synopsis of my date with Holly. "So, looks like that went well."

"Dude, it went great. I was totally not expecting for it to go that well."

"I bet! Just from an outsider looking in, you two seemed to really hit it off."

"Yeah, she's a cool girl."

"I'm guessing you're gonna see each other again?"

"Hopefully. I'm gonna text her tomorrow."

"You're not gonna wait a couple days and 'play it cool'? Ha ha."

"Fuck that. 'Cool' is for the emotionally weak who are afraid to take a stand."

"Ha. Well okay. I think I might have to agree with you on that."

Dane takes a drink from his scotch. After his gulp, he takes out his phone and works on a text message. I'm unable to make out what he's typing, but from over his shoulder I can tell he's sending the message to his ex-wife, who he still keeps in contact with. I guess I inspired him. Kate finishes channel surfing on the TV and lands on a rerun of *Saturday Night Live* from earlier this spring.

She walks up to Dane and me at the bar and addresses us. "You fellas want anything else to drink?"

"Yeah, I'll take a Coors Light."

"Dane?" asks Kate.

"I'm good for now," Dane replies.

"Come on," I say. "Have another drink. It's Saturday. Not like you have anywhere to be or anything to do tomorrow."

Dane caves. "Ahhh … okay. Fine. I'll do one more scotch and water."

"Alrighty … And, Matty, you're a bad influence," Kate teases.

"Hey, he's a grown man. He can make his own decisions."

"Ha ha. Yeah, I'm a big boy." Dane laughs.

"And if I was a bad influence, I'd suggest we do some lunchboxes."

"What's a lunchbox?" asks Dane.

"It's a drop shot I learned about during my days in Oklahoma. You take a third a glass of orange juice, a third a glass of Blue Moon, and you drop in a shot of amaretto."

"That sounds interesting," Dane hesitantly observes.

"It's fantastic. Trust me. You know, what the hell? Kate? Can we get two lunchboxes for Dane and me?"

"You sure about that?" Kate confirms.

"Yes, ma'am."

"Dane? You want one?" asks Kate.

"Ahh, what the hell. Yes, I'll take one too," Dane says, giving in.

"Okay. Be right back with those drinks," Kate says.

Kate walks away from Dane and me at the bar to prepare our drinks. As she mixes Dane's cocktail and uncaps my bottle of beer, Dane and I move our attention from conversation to the TV. *Saturday Night Live*'s *Weekend Update* segment is starting. Dane and I watch as the faux anchormen deliver social and political jokes relevant to month's prior. They're on a roll tonight, and every punch line is hitting with blunt force. Dane, Kate, and I can't help but laugh, despite many of the jokes falling into the category of dated. It's still amusing, and we appreciate the craft of the joke telling.

Kate returns, placing a scotch and water in front of Dane and a Coors Light longneck in front of me. She leaves our area again to prepare the lunchboxes. Dane and I cheers and suck at our beverages. I check the mountains on the bottle's label, and they remain as blue as ever. In fact, ever since Holly made her appearance, I've yet to taste a warm beer. I take it as a promising omen of things to come.

Kate comes back, this time holding two pint glasses, both containing Blue Moon beer and orange juice. Next, she pours out two shots of Amaretto and pushes them toward Dane and me at the bar. No coasters necessary for these drinks. They're going down quick.

"All right. There you boys go. I'm interested to see how this turns out," Kate announces.

Dane and I lift the shots of Amaretto and cheers the one-ounce glasses together.

"To our past downfalls. May we rise again," I toast.

Dane and I lower our shot glasses to the bar, reraise them, and drop them into the pints of Blue Moon and orange juice. The liquid turns murky and forms a reddish-orange color, resembling a tropical lake. Dane and I lift our pint glasses and, without hesitation, chug down the contents. The taste is sweet and tangy. The orange juice overpowers the beer, and the amaretto offers a sugary rush. I haven't had a Lunchbox in years, but the flavor takes my mind back to college when the world was my oyster, and potential was still currency. Kate and I look to Dane.

"So." *Burp*! "How was it?"

"I'm not gonna lie. That was fucking great, actually! Ha ha."

"I told you! It's the best drop shot on the market! The best kept secret!"

"You weren't lyin'."

"If it's that good, we may have to put it on the menu," Kate says.

"You totally should."

Kate gathers our empty pint and shot glasses and places them in the dishwasher near the kitchen. I pat Dane on the back, and he burps loudly, like an infant lacking self-awareness, and laughs. I can't help but chuckle myself. I take another drink of beer and fully cement my state of intoxication. The lunchbox has put me over the top, and now I feel immense joy. The kind that is only achieved when completely inebriated or completely in love. Those two circumstances have collided tonight, and I can't help but take notice of the pendulum of life swinging in the opposite direction for me. A zest for existence has returned. And now in the company of my comrade, Dane, I just want to spend as much time with my friend as possible, until it's time to say goodnight.

"Hey, Dane? You wanna have a smoke?"

"Yeah, sure. And after I finish my drink, I need to go."

"Of course. We can bring our drinks outside and finish them up there."

"Works for me," Dane says.

I pick my beer up and walk outside onto the patio. Dane hangs back and tabs out for the night with Kate. As I wait for Dane to exit the pub, I text Holly a sweet message for her to read before bed.

ME: I just wanted to say again how much fun I had tonight. I hope you got home safe.

I put my phone away and wait for Dane. After a couple of minutes, Dane exits the pub after leaving Kate a well-earned tip. He steps onto the patio, scotch and water in hand, and a glassy drunken look in his eyes. It's apparent he's good and proper fucked up at this juncture.

It's now Dane's final stand for the evening. He pauses after stepping outside and takes a deep breath of warm summer air. Kate stays inside watching *Saturday Night Live* reruns and laughs alone. I feel my phone vibrate. It's a message from Holly.

HOLLY. I had a great time tonight too. Just got home and about to go to bed. Talk to you tomorrow. Night, night. J

A smiley face emoji. I'm happy to see it.

32

Dane and I are outside on the patio. The summer breeze passes through the parking lot and onto the patio, and it is cooling. I haven't felt a wind current in the summer like this since I lived in the Great Plains. The breeze runs through the strip mall and grazes my arms, resulting in goose bumps—the welcomed kind. It's a perfect balance of hot and cold that only the summer, a late spring, or an early fall can achieve. There's a vibrancy in the atmosphere. I may be drunk off liquor and beer, or I'm still intoxicated from the encounter with Holly. "A woman's love can erase all fears" I was told once as a boy. I think my father said that, but it could've been a mixologist. I can't remember.

Dane removes two Camel Crush from the pack and hands me one. He puts his cigarette in his mouth and lights up. I place the Camel in between my lips and motion for the lighter. I'm gun-shy about using my lighter now. The fear of holding the Bic lighter I used to burn myself causes a slight panicked and tingly sensation to ripple through my hands, and I am uncomfortable. I allow the feeling to pass, and Dane passes me his lighter before holstering it back in his pocket. I flip my thumb over the metallic wheel and see the flame ignite. The end of my cigarette connects with the fiery blaze, and off

I am. It's been hours since I've ingested nicotine, and the soothing sensation overtakes me. My state of intoxication doubles, and my balance is affected. I step back and lean against the wrought iron fencing of the patio and hang like a scarecrow in a cornfield.

Dane takes pulls from the Camel and looks off into the night. He's aware that I'm still here but finds himself lost, checking his phone for return texts from his ex. No one has responded, much less her.

"Give it time."

"What?"

"She'll come around."

"Who? Matilda?"

"Yeah … Sure. Ha."

"Ha … Yeah. I wish she was still around. Especially on nights like these. You know?"

"Then why don't you go get her?"

"It's complicated, Matt. She's got baggage."

"So?"

"So, it has dictated how she navigates life. Including our marriage."

"Look. I'm not one to … comment on a marriage. But I think you're a good dude and deserve better."

"Ha. Well thanks for that. But I think Matilda is the only one for me. Do you think Holly is the only one for you?"

"Ha. Shit, man. I don't know. I just met her. But I think she's the closest to a shot in the arm I've felt in some years."

"That's how I feel about Matilda, Matt. It's all subjective to the person."

"I can see that."

Dane takes a long drag off his Camel and flicks the excess ash off the butt. The ash floats down to the pavement, gracefully and slowly. Not like a shooting star but more like an eclipse. Passing by at a glacial pace, only for a moment, just to be observed and gawked at by those fortunate enough to appreciate its presence. As I watch the ash float to street level, I take an equally long drag off my cigarette. I can't help but hope for Dane and others like us to find happiness in some form before last call.

Dane and I take pulls from our cigarettes. Dane slowly exhales his exhaust, while I blow smoke rings, trying to show off skills to a peanut gallery that has nut allergies and doesn't exist. I'm showing off for no one but myself. Dane finishes smoking his Camel, ashes it out on the bottom of his shoe, and flicks the butt into the parking lot. He pulls two more cigarettes from his pack and lights one up. He hands me the other cigarette. I accept and place it behind my ear like a stray pencil while I continue smoking the cigarette I've been working on.

"You know, Matt, I'm fifty-five, and I've been around a while—"

"You're fifty-five?"

"Yeah. Believe it or not, that's the truth. And I've seen some things."

"Oh, I bet."

"And what I've learned in these five or six decades of life is you can't pass on chances to be happy. You know, I … I had a chance at ultimate love … and she passed away. I watched her float down a river and drown. And I don't know if I'll ever get over that. I've tried. I tried with Matilda. But it … it just wasn't the same. At the end of the day, she wasn't my person. Even though I try to make it work to this day, to this moment. I texted her less than an hour ago, you see. And I know it isn't right, but … I just don't wanna be alone."

"You're not alone, man. You have Les and me and everyone here."

"It's not the same. We were supposed to be together forever. None of this was supposed to happen. We shouldn't know each other. You should be at home with a wife and kids and a mortgage— not living every day for the bar. I shouldn't be living every day for the bar. I should have children by now. I should be lecturing those kids about having grandkids. I should be writing a will to help pay for my grandkid's college fund, not … not smoking my life away on a patio with you. No offense."

"No, none taken."

"I just … I just should've gone after her. I should've tried harder. I should've done something. Then maybe she'd be alive. Then maybe I'd be alive."

A tear runs down Dane's face, and years' worth of emotions pour out. I can't help but feel sympathy. My eyes well up, yet I hold back. My own losses come back to me, and sympathy turns to empathy. I extend my arms outward and place a hand on Dane's shoulder. He returns the gesture and places a hand on my shoulder as well. Our grips tighten on the other's deltoid and then release. We back away from each other and take drags off our cigarettes—the longest drags each of us have ever taken. Mine is cashed, and I let it drop to the pavement. I step on the butt and twist my ankle, putting it out authoritatively. Dane exhales blue smoke from his lungs and watches it float out of his mouth into the ether.

"You're a good guy, Dane."

"You're not bad yourself, Matt."

"And you have people. You're not alone."

"Thanks. I just want to say … if you love this girl, and you believe there's something there, don't waste time. Don't let her find some other guy. Let her know how you feel … and you know, just be *the* guy."

"It's still early, but I know what you're saying. I will, Dane."

"Just make sure you don't let the moments slip."

"I won't. I think there are more moments to come."

"I hope so, Matty."

Dane takes an extended drag off his cigarette until there's nothing left to puff. Once he's done, he flicks the cigarette off into the parking lot, and we watch it float to the ground, landing on a speed bump. The butt doesn't roll or bounce. It just stops in place.

Maybe we're all just discarded cigarette butts floating to our speed bumps, I think. Runaway vehicles with no destination in sight. Only slowed by life or circumstance or coincidence. Left to gear up and press on after an inevitable break. Maybe the time at the Royal Tree has been a speed bump. Maybe this is purgatory. Maybe we're all just waiting for angels to bring us home. Or maybe, we're just all alone, and this is hell.

I refuse to accept this theory. I met my angel tonight, and she's real. I want to come home. I want her to bring me home. *Please save me from this eternal summer*, I beg myself. *No more nights in the darkness*, I plead. It's time to make my escape.

"All right. It's time for me to go, Matt."

"All right, Dane. You good to drive?"

"Yeah. I'll be fine."

"Okay. It was good hanging out with you, Dane. You're a good dude."

"Good hanging out with you too, Matty. Be here tomorrow?"

"We'll have to see. But I'd have to say … maybe."

"Ha. Okay. See you then."

"See ya, Dane."

Dane exits the patio and walks through the parking lot toward his car. I watch him as he leaves, making sure there's no sign of stumbling or police in the vicinity. Dane reaches his green Honda Element and climbs in. The car engine starts, and Dane pulls out of the parking space, driving off toward home. I'm jealous of him. I'm jealous he had someone that hurt so much to lose. I hope he gets home safe. I hope I have someone to see tomorrow.

Before leaving the patio for the bar, I notice an old mint-green Cadillac El Dorado sitting in an otherwise vacant parking lot, with the exception of Kate's Mercury Cougar. I don't remember seeing the Cadillac in the parking lot when I escorted Holly to her Uber. Maybe it was left there by someone who was too drunk to drive home from the movie theater next door? They do serve alcohol there after all. No matter. I think I'll go back inside for a night cap before hoofing it home.

33

Inside the Royal Tree, I sit at a new stool, smack-dab in the middle of the bar, facing the TV. Center stage. I watch the remainder of *Saturday Night Live* with Kate and occasionally take pulls from a bottle of Coors Light. The mountains are as blue as ever.

The final skits of the night air and conclude a worthy effort on the part of the cast and crew. Kate and I watch as the cast, host, and musical guest share the stage to wave goodbye to the audience at the end of the show. They hug and congratulate one another on a job well done. It's a heartwarming scene that brings to mind saying goodbye and see you later to my own friends. And Holly.

At the conclusion of the show, Kate switches off the TV and cleans up the pub. It's just a few minutes past 1:00 a.m., and I'm the lone customer remaining. She knows I won't mind if she tidies up around me.

"Closing up early tonight?"

"Yeah, it's looking like that. Don't feel rushed though. I won't do last call for another half hour or so."

"Okay, cool. Care for some music?"

"Yeah, go ahead, honey. You have enough cash to play something?"

"Umm, yeah I got a few bucks left."

"Well, have at it then."

I stand up from the stool and stagger toward the jukebox. The booze is operating my human machine now. I reach the jukebox without incident and struggle to focus on the screen. I remove a crinkled wad of dollar bills from my pocket and attempt to insert them into the music box. Every dollar is rejected, with the jukebox spitting the bills out as quickly as it takes them in. The bills are too wrinkled for the jukebox to accept them. This is the first example of rejection I've experienced all day, which makes the matter even more frustrating. Has my luck run dry?

Not to be defied, I run the length of the dollars over the edge of the jukebox machine, flattening them out, desperately seeking to remove the wrinkles from the tender. I have success with ironing out a couple of the bills and reinsert them into the machine. They're accepted this go-round, and a sense of accomplishment is reinstalled in my being.

I scan the jukebox song library for tuneage. I'd search for songs outside the library, but given my state and inability to properly focus my eyes or efficiently use my motor functions, I err on the side of compromise. Two dollars are in the machine and there are four songs to choose. I make my selections—"Linger" by the Cranberries, "Stand By Me" by Ben E. King, "Will You Still Love Me Tomorrow" by the Shirelles, and "Again" by Lenny Kravitz. Love songs feel like a proper way to send off the night.

I stagger back toward the bar and plop onto a bar stool. I listen attentively to the music pulsating from the PA system. Something about the lyrics is resonating more so now than they had in the past. Maybe it's true that you can only truly appreciate a love song when you're in love. The same way you can only fully grasp the pain in a depressing song when you yourself are in emotional turmoil. Makes sense to me. With this realization, I sing the lyrics softly, uninhibited and confident in the message. Kate laughs at my vocal performance before she joins in, singing along in unison. For the rest of the playlist, we harmonize with the tracks as Kate mops the floor around me. And then I order one more beer before last call.

34

Kate finishes mopping the floor and stacking the chairs on top of the tables scattered around the pub. The other bar stools are pushed in close to the bar and wiped clean with Lysol. I take my time drinking my beer, savoring the last sips before I'm forced to exit and make the half-mile walk home to my apartment. I imagine my cat is waiting for me, sitting on the windowsill looking out at God knows what, wondering when I'll be back to scratch his head and tease him with a toy mouse on a string. I'm looking forward to seeing him too.

I drink from the beer bottle and rub my thumb over the label, amazed that, for years, the bottle has been my long-standing mistress. And now I feel a sense of guilt in cheating on it with a woman. Holly. It's a necessary affair. A man can only be left in a solitary state for so long before inevitably breaking out of his shell. Even a hermit crab leaves its shell after a while. And I'm now happy to leave a life of loneliness and emotional solitude for one that offers the possibility of a future with a companion by my side. A partner in crime. An angel to replace the demon I lean on. I'm looking forward to texting Holly tomorrow.

Kate is back behind the bar waiting for me to finish my beer so she can leave. I sense her urgency and take larger gulps of beer.

Kate leans against the bar and faces me. "You have a good night?"

"Yeah. Yeah, I did actually. How about you?"

"Eh, not bad. It's been interesting. That's for sure."

"Just another night at the Royal Tree, huh?"

"You could say that. But something tells me the piss-stained window outside might have left a mark on us. Ha ha." Kate laughs, addressing the incident with the homeless woman hours ago.

"Ha, yeah, but shockingly that was probably only the third strangest thing to happen here today."

"Occupational hazards. They're a bitch. So, looked like you liked that girl in here earlier. Holly? Is that her name?"

"Yeah, Holly. I mean, yeah. I liked her a lot actually."

"I can tell by the songs you've been playing in here since she left."

"Ha. Oh, you're gonna give me shit about that now?"

"Ha. Just an observation. You gonna bring her around some more?"

"I'd like to. If she'll have me."

"She will. I'm a woman. We have a sense for these things. I think she liked you quite a bit. Just don't screw it up."

"What makes you think I'd screw it up?"

"Ha. I'm just teasing, honey. She seems like a sweet girl. You be nice to her."

"Hey, I'm always nice."

"As long as you don't have too much whiskey in you, or your name isn't Baby Baby."

"Ha. What about Baby Baby?"

"Like I don't know about what happened earlier. I know everything around here, Matty."

"Ha. All-seeing, all-knowing, huh?"

"Don't forget it. And don't let anything like that Baby Baby incident happen around here again, okay?"

"Sorry about that. I'll do my best. It was just … well, you know."

"No, I know. Desperate times and all that. Between you and me, you did the right thing. But as far as everyone else is concerned, I know nothing about that. Okay?"

"Got it. Thanks for letting me stick around after. I appreciate it."

"You're always welcome here, Matty. Except for … right about now. It's time for me to close up."

"Yeah, I guess it's about that time."

I suck down the remainder of my beer and hand the empty bottle back to Kate. She tosses the empty longneck in the garbage and tabs me out for the evening. The tab is a funny thing. I have no idea how much it will be, but it's always more than expected, and I'm always left feeling the punishment doesn't fit the crime. Everything has a markup—especially when it comes to a good time. But it's hard to be upset when you know the cost associated going in. It's like finding oneself upset about contracting lung cancer after smoking for thirty years. It's to be expected.

The bar tab is no different. The bar tab is like the way Christians believe God keeps track of everything you've done in your life up until the point you die. And then on judgment day, you're left to stand in front of your maker as he decides your ultimate fate. In the case of the way the bar punishes you for your ingestions, you can either have enough cash or credit to pay the tab and go home feeling great, or you can come up empty-handed and be banished forever, or at least sentenced to the kitchen to wash dishes until your penance is paid. Either way, you owe something in return. And it's going to be more than you wish.

Kate prints out the bill for the evening and places it in front of me. As expected, it's more than I figured—over a hundred dollars. My eyes bulge and then squint a bit as I struggle to read the check and make sure it's correct. It is. I hand over my credit card to Kate, and she swipes it in the machine, officially paying my debt to the Royal Tree for the evening. Knowing I spent that amount of money in here today on drinks feels like I've been sent to a financial hell.

But fuck it. I had fun getting there. I'll take my lumps and keep on moving, until the next time.

I leave Kate a thirty-dollar tip, and she thanks me. She knows I don't have the money to leave such hefty gratuity, but she takes the money anyway. She's earned it. I stand from my bar stool and push it in toward the bar and wave goodbye to Kate.

"Kate, I am now headed out."

"All right, honey. Thanks for coming in. You want a ride home? I'll be locking up here in about ten more minutes."

"Hmm. Ah you know what? I'm just gonna go ahead and walk home. It's less than a mile from here."

"You sure? It's no trouble."

"Yeah, I'm sure. It's a nice night out. I figure I'll take it all in."

"Okay then. Well, have a good night, Matt. And get home safe."

"I will, Kate. Bye-bye."

"Bye, honey."

And with that, I gingerly walk to the front door of the Royal Tree and exit for the night. I step off the patio and into the parking lot and pause. It's a beautiful night, and I stare up at the stars, contemplating the vastness of the cosmos. Something is in the air, and I can't quite put my finger on it. And right now, I really don't care. I don't wish to assume an epiphany has hit me, but there is a notion of healthy nihilism I'm feeling, and it's as intoxicating as my favorite bourbon. I no longer care about my financial troubles. I no longer care about my loneliness. I no longer care about the people I've lost in the past. I no longer care about wondering when my next paycheck is going to come. I no longer care about whether Holly will like me. I no longer care about the bar tab. I no longer care about a lack of faith.

I have no worries regarding anything as I stand in the parking lot outside the Royal Tree. A silent calm overshadows my troubles. I no longer care about anything because it feels like I have everything now—job prospects, friends, community, a woman, a cat, a home, a hereafter. It's hard to believe how much my perspective has changed in the span of a day, but it has. No longer does the glass look half-empty. It now looks as if there's even more left to drink. Even more left to enjoy. There's so much more than there once seemed to be. I guess I can reflect and say this may have been the greatest day of my life.

Before I step forward and navigate through the parking lot, I continue to pause and stare out at the stars and the city skyline off in the distance. It used to seem so far away, yet now it appears just in arm's reach. A city that I had lusted after for so long now is just nothing more than well-lit buildings illuminating the sky. If I was chasing after urban zest all this time, would I have met Dane and Les and Kate and Tyler and Holly and Baby Baby even? Would I have had this glorious day? Would I have found hope? Would I have found acceptance? This I cannot answer fully, but I do know I did find all this in a suburban strip mall parking lot. Sometimes the answers are right in front of you. You just have to open your eyes and your mind. And they may just pop out and surprise you every now and again.

I take my first steps through the parking lot, and I can't help but think of how much I'm looking forward to getting home to my cat and playing records and possibly calling Bob or Ernie to tell them about the date with Holly. I contemplate what record I'm going to listen to first at home. Definitely something from the Motown era. That's the mood I'm feeling and the one I wish to ride out until I eventually pass out in my bed or on the couch, nestled up with my furry feline friend.

I ruminate on what I'm going to say to Holly tomorrow. A number of possible opening lines come to mind, but they all seem too forward. Too desperate. I'm going to have to let it come to me. Going to have to sleep on it. Maybe the words of Motown heroes immortalized on my records will provide some inspiration. I just want her to know how much I wish to see her again. That day cannot come soon enough.

I walk through the parking lot and pass by the only two cars left—Kate's Mercury Cougar and the old Cadillac El Dorado. I feel present in the moment and listen to my feet hit the pavement, rhythmically. It sounds like a percussive beat I'm playing with my extremities. I hum the words to one of the songs Holly played in the pub before she left.

As I sing to myself, I hear a car door open behind me. I assume it's Kate climbing into her Mercury Cougar on her way home. I stop in my tracks and pivot around to see the source of the noise. Kate is nowhere in sight. Instead, I'm met face-to-face again with Baby Baby, standing outside the Cadillac El Dorado. Suddenly, I connect the dots and realize it was him who had been parked outside throughout the night. Maybe he just sobered up and came back for his car.

"Baby Baby, is that you?" I ask nervously.

No reply. He just stands there next to the driver's side of the mint-green El Dorado and broods. His face is busted, and his eyes are black from the beating he took earlier. There's a bandage taped across his nose and tissues in his nostrils. I would also assume there could be ice on his balls, but it's too dark in the dimly lit parking lot to accurately make such an assessment.

I call out to him again. "Baby Baby? What are you doing out here?"

Still no answer. I stay put and consider turning and running. But from what? A middle-aged man who's most assuredly walking with a hindered gait? I try to remain calm, but Baby Baby's silence is disconcerting.

"Do you need something, Baby Baby? It's over. We handled our shit earlier."

"It's not over yet, you sum bitch." He speaks in that unmistakable southern Louisiana drawl.

"So, what? Huh? You come back for what?"

Baby Baby grunts, and I see his face turn from a look of frustration to one of malice. He steps forward. I freeze for a moment and decide not to run. A confidence in handling him physically is instilled in me from earlier in the night, and I'm aware I'll have to defend myself once more. So, I step toward him. Baby Baby halts his glacial charge and turns himself to the side. I keep pressing forward until I'm within a few feet of him. Baby Baby quickly turns his body back toward me and is holding something black and metallic in his right hand. A pistol.

Before I can think about turning and running home or to anywhere resembling shelter, I hear it. A loud bang, like fireworks, echoes throughout the empty parking lot. Neither of us moves. I feel an immense amount of pressure in my stomach and look down to my abdomen. Blood slowly runs out of an open wound. The son of a bitch shot me. I place my hands over the bloody hole, fall back on my butt, and lay out on my back. A number of ideas fly into my brain like a swarm of bees, each carrying its own train of thought. I land on one singular notion and wonder, *Is this it?*

Baby Baby stands for a brief moment, stunned in place at what he's just done. He soon backpedals toward the mint-green El Dorado and climbs in, hastily starting the engine. I see his headlights illuminate, and music blares out of the rolled-down car window. For some reason, all I can think to do is make out what the song is playing through Baby Baby's radio.

The car pulls out of its parking space and drives forward in a rush. I look up at the sky and can only think as I listen to the music pumping from the car. It's an old song I've heard before. The car passes away, and the music fades out in the distance. As I lay alone bleeding in the parking lot I've walked through so many times before, I realize what song it is. And I finally know what I'd like to tell Holly tomorrow.

CPSIA information can be obtained
at www.ICGtesting.com
Printed in the USA
BVHW071029071220
595086BV00003B/385